CRITICS CHEER
JULIE GARWOOD'S
FOR THE ROSES

"Ms. Garwood combines the Old West and England to create an incredibly entrancing tale with a cast of unique characters that will certainly linger in your heart. Her gifted prose is always a treat, and *FOR THE ROSES* is no exception."

—*Rendezvous*

"An enchanting tale with a happy ending . . ."

—*Abilene Reporter-News*

"A powerful story about four urchin boys who rescue a baby in New York City, it's filled with characters you'll never forget."

—*Romantic Reader News*

"Lively and charming . . . Filled with humor and appealing characters . . ."

—*Library Journal*

"[A] page-turner filled with lots of family values . . . the reader is never out of Garwood's skillful comfort zone."

—*Kirkus Reviews*

"As wild as the Old West . . . "

—*Publishers Weekly*

"There will be moments when you'll laugh and cry, and others when the warmth and love captured here will enfold you in its powerful embrace. With a master's pen, Julie Garwood explores the heart and soul of a family whose love and loyalty will truly inspire. *FOR THE ROSES* is a brilliant ach

—*~~~~antic Times*

D1052280

Books by Julie Garwood

Gentle Warrior
Rebellious Desire
Honor's Splendour
The Lion's Lady
The Bride
Guardian Angel
The Gift
The Prize
The Secret
Castles
Saving Grace
Prince Charming
For the Roses
The Wedding
One Pink Rose
One White Rose
One Red Rose

Published by POCKET BOOKS

JULIE GARWOOD

One Red Rose

POCKET BOOKS
New York   London   Toronto   Sydney   Tokyo   Singapore

Letters to Julie Garwood
should be addressed to:

P.O. Box 7574
Leawood, KS 66211

or her Web site:

http://www.juliegarwood.com

This book is a work of fiction. Names, characters, places and
incidents are products of the author's imagination or are used
fictitiously. Any resemblance to actual events or locales or persons,
living or dead, is entirely coincidental.

An *Original* Publication of POCKET BOOKS

 POCKET BOOKS, a division of Simon & Schuster Inc.
1230 Avenue of the Americas, New York, NY 10020

ISBN: 0-671-01010-7

First Pocket Books printing August 1997

10 9 8 7 6 5 4 3 2 1

POCKET and colophon are registered trademarks of
Simon & Schuster Inc.

Printed in the U.S.A.

Prologue

❧

*L*ong ago there lived a remarkable family. They were the Clayborne brothers, and they were held together by bonds far stronger than blood.

They met when they were boys living on the streets in New York City. Runaway slave Adam, pickpocket Douglas, gunslinger Cole, and con man Travis survived by protecting one another from the older gangs roaming the city. When they found an abandoned baby girl in their alley, they vowed to make a better life for her and headed west.

They eventually settled on a piece of land they named Rosehill, deep in the heart of Montana Territory.

The only guidance they received as they were growing up came from the letters of Adam's mother, Rose. Rose learned about the children from their heartfelt letters to her, for they confided their fears, their hopes and their dreams, and in return she gave them what they had never had before, a mother's unconditional love and acceptance.

In time, each came to know her as his own Mama Rose.

After twenty long years, Rose joined them. Her sons and daughter were finally content. Her arrival was indeed a cause for both celebration and consternation. Her daughter was married to a fine man and recently gave birth to a beautiful baby girl, and her sons had grown to be honorable, strong men, each successful in his own right. Travis and Douglas had married well. But Mama Rose wasn't quite satisfied just yet. Adam and Cole had become too settled in their bachelor ways to suit her. Since she believed God helps those who help themselves, there was only one thing left for her to do.

She was going to meddle.

Time of Roses

It was not in the Winter
Our loving lot was cast;
It was the time of roses—
We pluck'd them as we pass'd!

That churlish season never frown'd
On early lovers yet:
O no—the world was newly crown'd
With flowers when first we met!

'Twas twilight, and I bade you go,
But still you held me fast;
It was the time of roses—
We pluck'd them as we pass'd!

—Thomas Hood (1798–1845)

One

❦

Rosehill Ranch, Montana Valley, Spring, 1881

He found her in his bed.

Adam Clayborne surprised his family by coming home in the dead of night two days earlier than expected. He hadn't planned to return to the ranch until Friday, but his business was finished, and he was sick and tired of sleeping outdoors. He wanted clean sheets and a soft mattress underneath him.

He knew the house was packed to capacity, for next weekend was Mama Rose's birthday, and his brothers and sister had all agreed to come back to the homestead early to help with the preparations. Most of the town of Blue Belle was invited to the shindig, along with twenty or thirty people from as far away as Hammond. Mama Rose had made a good number of friends since she'd taken up residence at the ranch a little over a year ago. There were more than fifty men and women in her church group alone, and every one of them was planning to attend the celebration.

By the time Adam had bedded down his horse and

gotten a cool drink in the kitchen, it was well after midnight. The house was as quiet as a church on Saturday night. He removed his boots in the foyer and tried not to make any noise as he crept up the stairs, went into his bedroom at the end of the hall, and began to undress. He didn't bother to turn up the lamp on the night stand because the moonlight streaming in through the open window was sufficient for him to make out the contours of the furniture.

He tossed his shirt on a nearby chair, stretched his arms wide, and yawned. Lord, it was good to be home. Bone weary and half asleep, he sank down on the double bed to take off his socks—except he didn't actually sit on the bed. He sat down on a very soft, warm, sweet-scented woman.

She let out a loud groan. He let out a blasphemy.

Genevieve Perry had been sound asleep one second and was wide awake the next. She felt as though the house had just caved in on her. Instinctively she shoved the dead weight off of her legs and bolted upright in the bed. Grabbing hold of the sheets, she held them up to her neck and peered over at the huge man sprawled out on the floor.

"What *are* you doing?" she whispered.

"I'm trying to get into my bed," he whispered back. "Adam?"

"Yes, Adam. Who are you?"

She swung her long legs over the side of the bed and put her hand out to him.

"My name's Genevieve, and it's such a pleasure to meet you. Your mother's told me so much about you."

His eyes widened in disbelief. He almost laughed, so ludicrous was the situation. Didn't the woman realize he could see her bare arms and legs? She obviously didn't have much on, and that sheet was a paltry barrier at best.

"I'll be happy to shake your hand when you're dressed."

"Oh . . . Lord."

Her reaction told him she'd finally recognized the awkwardness of their circumstances.

"I guess turning the lamp up is out of the question," he said.

"No, no, we can't do that. I'm in my nightgown. You really should get out of my room before anyone finds you here. This isn't appropriate."

"It's my room," he reminded her. "And lower your voice, or you'll wake the entire household. I don't want my brothers running in here to find out what's going on."

"Nothing's going on."

"I'm aware of that, Genevieve." He sat up, untangled his long legs, and braced his arms on his knees. He tried to be patient as he waited for her to explain why she was in his bed.

Her vision finally adjusted to the darkness, and she got a good look at the man she had been dreaming about for the past two years. Lord, he was gorgeous. She had tried to picture him in her mind, had fantasized about him too, but now she realized she hadn't done the man justice. The angles of his face were perfectly sculptured. He looked as though he had been molded from one of the ancient statues she'd seen in the museum back home. Adam had the same square forehead and high cheekbones and the identical straight nose and mouth. His eyes made him even more beautiful. They were the color of midnight. His gaze was intensely focused on her now, and she could feel the heat all the way down to her toes.

She couldn't stop staring at him. He was much bigger than she'd imagined him to be, and far more muscular. He was lean, yet his upper arms were enormous, suggesting amazing strength. She could feel the coiled tension in him and knew, without a doubt, that if he decided to pounce on her, it would happen before she had time to blink. The thought made her shiver. She'd never imagined that he would be dangerous, but then she'd never pictured him frowning, and he was certainly frowning now.

And she looked like a poor, frumpy relative. She was wearing an old, faded nightgown, a favorite she refused to throw away because it was so comfortable. She pulled the sheet up higher to hide the frayed neckline.

She should have been horrified by his intrusion. She wasn't though. She wasn't the least bit afraid. Why, she wouldn't be feeling the most irresistible urge to laugh if she were afraid, would she? Besides, she knew Adam better than anyone else in the whole world, even his brothers, because she had read all the letters he'd written over the years to his Mama Rose.

"You don't have to worry," she whispered. "I'm not going to shout for help. I know who you are and I'm not afraid."

He clenched his jaw tight. "You don't have any reason to be afraid. What are you doing in my bed?"

"The guest room's occupied, so your mother told me to take your room. I surprised her by showing up without giving her any advance warning. She invited me to come to Rosehill a long time ago, but due to circumstances beyond my control, I couldn't get here until now."

It suddenly dawned on him exactly who Genevieve was. Adam was a big man, but he could be quick when he wanted to be. He was on his feet and halfway across the room before she had time to draw another breath.

She grabbed her robe from the foot of the bed and quickly put it on. She started to stand up but changed her mind almost immediately. She didn't want him to get the notion that she was chasing after him.

"Wait," she called out. "Didn't your mother tell you I was coming to Rosehill?"

"No."

Adam knew he sounded surly. He couldn't help that. He should have known who she was right away. Her southern accent should have been a dead give-away, and although he'd certainly noticed the soft, musical lilt in her voice, it hadn't occurred to him until this moment that Genevieve was the woman his Mama Rose had told him about.

He was reaching for the doorknob when she called out to him again. "Do you mean to say she didn't explain?"

He slowly turned around. "Explain what?" he hedged.

She pulled her robe close about her and moved into the moonlight. He saw her face clearly then, and in that moment, Adam realized the jeopardy he was in. Without a doubt, Genevieve Perry was the most beautiful woman he had ever seen. Her dark hair was cropped short and framed a heart-shaped, angelic face. She had high cheek bones, a narrow nose, and a mouth that could drive a man to imagine all sorts of things. Her skin was flawless, and that innocent smile of hers could cause real havoc.

His gaze moved lower and, Lord help him, her long, shapely legs were as perfect as the rest of her.

He broke out in a cold sweat. She was beautiful all right, and he couldn't wait to be rid of her.

"What exactly was Mama Rose supposed to explain?"

She smiled once again, a heart-stopping smile. Every nerve in his body was warning him to get out of there before it was too late and he was captured in her enchanting spell.

"Adam, I'm your bride."

He didn't panic, but he came close. He nearly ripped the door off its hinges when he opened it, but escape was impossible. His brothers Travis and Cole were blocking the entrance. The two of them came rushing into the bedroom to find out what all the commotion was. Both men were bare-chested, barefoot, and wide awake. Travis had his gun out and was looking for a target.

"What the . . ." Cole came to a dead stop when Adam gave him a hard shove.

"Put your damned gun away, Travis," Adam ordered.

"We heard a crash in here," Cole said.

"I fell on the floor," Adam whispered.

Both brothers looked incredulous. Travis was the first to smile. "You fell on the floor? How in God's name did you do that?"

"Never mind," Adam muttered.

Travis elbowed his way past his brothers so he could see Genevieve. "Are you all right?"

"Of course she's all right," Adam answered.

"What are you doing home so soon?" Cole asked.

"Get off my foot," Adam snapped.

Cole took a step back and then asked, "What are you doing in Genevieve's room?"

"It's my bedroom," Adam reminded him. "No one told me she'd be sleeping in my bed."

Cole smiled. "Well, now, that had to be a real nice surprise."

"Gentlemen, will you please leave?" Genevieve called out.

She was immediately sorry she'd said a word, for she'd inadvertently drawn attention to herself. All three brothers turned to her. She tried to scrunch down under the sheets and disappear.

Cole walked forward. "Adam didn't scare you, did he?"

The brother had almost reached the bed when she bolted upright. "Do you mind, Cole?"

He stopped. "Mind what? You aren't embarrassed, are you?"

"You've got your robe on," Travis reminded her. "And after living with us for a week, you've got to know you're perfectly safe."

"Is anyone hungry?" Cole asked.

"I could eat something," Travis said. "What about you, Genevieve?"

"No, thank you."

Adam gritted his teeth in frustration. He couldn't wait to get his brothers out in the hallway so he could give them a piece of his mind.

"You two haven't been properly introduced, have you?" Travis said. He crossed the room to stand next to Cole. "One of us ought to introduce them to each other, and now is as good a time as any."

"For the love of . . ." Adam began.

"Stop teasing your brother . . ." Genevieve said at the very same time. The laughter in her voice indicated she wasn't the least bit upset.

"This will only take a minute," Travis insisted. "Genevieve, I'd like you to meet the oldest and the meanest of the Clayborne brothers. His name is John Quincy Adam Clayborne, but everyone calls him Adam. Adam, I'd like you to meet Miss Genevieve Perry, who came here all the way from New Orleans, Louisiana. You should get to know her as soon as possible, since the wedding plans are already in the works. Good night, Genevieve. See you in the morning."

"Good night," she replied.

Adam wasn't amused by his brothers' antics. He pushed Cole and Travis out into the hallway, pulled the door closed, and then demanded to know what Genevieve was doing there.

"Mama Rose invited her to come here," Travis explained.

"But that was over a year ago. Why did she decide to come to Rosehill now?"

Cole shrugged. "Maybe it wasn't convenient before or she had something else she had to do first. Does it matter?"

Adam shook his head. Now, he decided, wasn't the time to get into a long discussion. "Where am I supposed to sleep?"

"The guest room's out," Cole said, "unless you want to sleep with our nephew. Parker's teething, and he'll wake you up around four in the morning."

"Why can't the baby sleep in with his parents?"

"Mama Rose thought Douglas and Isabelle could use a little privacy," Travis explained with a yawn. "Genevieve's pretty, isn't she? And don't tell me you didn't notice."

Adam let out a sigh. "I noticed."

He started down the steps, but Cole stopped him with a question. "What are you going to do about her?"

"I'm not going to do anything about her."

"She came here to marry you," Cole whispered. "At least that's what Mama Rose told us, and when she suggested a June wedding, Genevieve didn't argue."

"What a mess," Adam muttered.

"I'm going back to bed," Cole announced.

Travis followed Adam down to the foyer. "We really like her, Adam. If you'll open your mind to the idea, I think you'll like her too. She's got a great sense of humor, and you should hear her sing. She's amazing. If you'll only get to know her before you make any decisions, you'll—"

"I'm not marrying her."

"Adam, you don't have to do anything you don't want to do."

"Why didn't one of you let me know she was here?"

"How could we let you know? You've been camping, remember?" Travis said.

"You had a week to find me."

"Why are you in such a foul mood? No one's going to hold a gun to your head and make you marry her."

"I'm going to bed."

He ended up in the bunkhouse. A half hour later, he was still trying to get comfortable on a narrow, lumpy mattress. He was too big for the bed. His feet hung over the edge, and he couldn't turn over without flinging himself to the floor.

He doubted he would get much sleep anyway, as thoughts of Genevieve kept intruding. He stacked his hands behind his head and thought about the situation. His mother's interference in his life was galling, and what in the name of God was he going to do about the mess she had created? Surely Genevieve didn't really expect to marry him just because Mama Rose had suggested the idea to her. Nowadays, most women balked at an arranged marriage, and what son in his right mind would let his mother choose his bride for him?

Adam knew it was going to be up to him to make Genevieve understand that marriage was out of the question. He would sit her down and have a long talk with her. Yes, that's what he was going to have to do. He would tell her that he had made his mind up a long time ago that he was meant to live alone. He was too set in his ways, liked solitude, and hated distraction of any kind. In other words, he wasn't husband material. Family was the only disruption he allowed. His brothers were rarely at Rosehill now, and since his sister, Mary Rose, had had the baby, Mama Rose spent most of her time with her new granddaughter. Mary Rose's husband, Harrison, had built a home on the edge of Blue Belle to accommodate the three women in his life, and Mama Rose much preferred town life over the isolation of the ranch.

Adam wasn't a recluse. There were always at least twenty hired hands to supervise, so his days were quite busy, and he didn't mind returning to the big empty house at night alone. In fact, he liked it. Admittedly, his life had become a little too structured and orderly to suit most people, but he was content, and that was all that mattered. When he was younger, he'd longed to see the world, but he'd given up on that foolish dream years ago and now traveled from one exotic port to another through the books he read. Cole accused him of acting like an old man. Adam didn't disagree with his brother's evaluation. He had always been happy with his life, and he would be happy again just as soon as he straightened out this misunderstanding.

He decided to wait until after the birthday celebration to talk to Genevieve. He would be kind, but forceful, as he explained his position.

Her expectations were unreasonable, and he hoped that after he'd had his say, she would realize he was right. He didn't want to hurt her, and he certainly wasn't looking forward to a confrontation. He wasn't a cruel man who took delight in breaking women's hearts, but he would do what was necessary to avert a disaster, no matter how distraught she became.

He hoped to God she wouldn't cry or become hysterical. Regardless, he would stand firm. Adam fell asleep convinced that eventually Genevieve would get over him.

Two

🙠🙢

She couldn't possibly marry him, and just as soon as she could get him alone for a few minutes, she would tell him so. She wasn't in a position to marry anyone now, not with all the trouble hanging over her head, but she wasn't about to go into a lengthy explanation when she talked to Adam. She would simply tell him that marriage was out of the question. Then she would be on her way.

Admittedly, before things had become so horribly complicated and bleak, she had entertained the notion of marrying him. After she had read all of his letters, she'd even dreamed about it, but then the Reverend Ezekiel Jones came into her life and turned it upside down. Because of her own naiveté and self-involvement, she could no longer consider becoming the wife of such an honorable man as Adam Clayborne.

It was her hope that once she had completed the dreaded duty of explaining her change of heart to

Adam, she would gain a little peace of mind. Lord only knew, she was due for some.

She needed privacy for their talk though, and privacy wasn't easily accomplished at Rosehill these days. The two-story house was bursting at the seams with returning family members and their spouses and babies. Adam was constantly surrounded by his relatives, and there was also a steady procession of friends, and strangers too, who stopped by the ranch for a cool drink, a hot meal, and a little conversation. None of the Claybornes ever turned anyone away.

As head of the household, Adam tried to be hospitable. He also tried to avoid her whenever possible. It hadn't taken her any time at all to come to that conclusion, for every time she entered a room he happened to be in, he found a reason to get up and leave. His abrupt departures would have bothered her if she hadn't already surmised from his wary glances that he was as uncomfortable with the situation as she was.

Time was running out and she would have to leave soon. She had made a promise, and she was determined to keep it. She had already stayed at Rosehill much longer than she had originally intended, and she was feeling tremendously guilty about deceiving all of the Claybornes. She had come there under false pretenses to hide, and every time she looked at dear Mama Rose, Genevieve's shoulders slumped a little more from the weight of all her lies.

The Clayborne family had made her feel worse by being so good to her. They had welcomed her into their home and treated her as though she belonged there. Mama Rose constantly sang her praises. She told her family that Genevieve was a sweet, generous person with high moral standards. Genevieve wondered how Mama Rose would feel about her if she knew the truth.

The opportunity to talk to Adam in private finally presented itself on the day of Mama Rose's birthday celebration. As Genevieve was coming down the stairs to the first floor, she spotted Adam going into his library, and, saints be praised, he was all alone. She straightened her shoulders, gathered her resolve, and hurried after him.

Two hours later, she was still trying to get to the library. First she had been waylaid by his sister, Mary Rose, who asked her to please supervise the men putting up the picnic tables while Mary Rose fed and changed her daughter. Over the past week, Genevieve had become very close to Mary Rose, and she was happy to help out. An hour later she had only just completed the task when Adam's brother Douglas asked her to please hold his ten-month-old son, Parker, while he helped construct the platform that would be used by the band Travis had hired.

Parker was a little charmer, and Genevieve certainly didn't mind taking care of him. The baby was persnickety with almost everyone but her. He was going through what his parents referred to as "a shy phase," which meant he usually started screaming whenever a stranger came within ten feet of him. He'd taken quite a fancy to Genevieve though, and much to his parents' surprise, the moment he'd spotted her, he'd put his arms out and demanded with a grunt that she pick him up. She was wearing a colorful necklace at the time, and she was convinced Parker only put up with her so that he could get to the trinket he thought he might like to eat.

Genevieve considered taking the curly-headed cherub with her to the library to talk to Adam, then changed her mind. Parker was fretful and would have been too much of a distraction. With all the pounding and shouting and laughing, she also knew that if she tried to put him in his crib, he'd have none of it. So she carried him out to the porch, sat down in the rocker Douglas had carried out for her, and let the baby rest against her chest and watch the chaos.

A shrill whistle made Parker jump. She soothed him with a gentle pat and a whispered word.

"Harrison, we could use your help," Cole shouted. "Bring Adam with you."

The screen door opened and Mary Rose's husband came out. He had his daughter, Victoria, in the crook of his arm. He looked a bit guilty as he came across the porch to stand in front of her. Genevieve knew what he wanted before he asked. She shifted Parker to the left side of her lap so there would be enough room for his adorable seven-month-old cousin.

"Would you mind holding Victoria for a few minutes while I help build the platform?" he asked in his rich Scottish brogue. "She's been fed and changed. My wife's helping in the kitchen, but if you don't think . . ."

"I can manage," she insisted.

Harrison got his daughter settled next to Parker, patted both babies, then removed his jacket and tossed it on the railing on his way down the steps.

Genevieve had her hands full. Parker was determined to gnaw on Victoria's arm, but Genevieve gently pulled her arm away and substituted his blanket. His thumb immediately went into his mouth, and he began to make loud slurping noises.

Travis came running up the steps. The sight of his nephew and niece snuggled together in her arms made him smile.

"You sure do have a way with babies."

"It would seem so," she agreed. She burst out laughing then, for her little charges looked up at her and smiled. Both babies were drooling.

"They're perfect, aren't they?" she said.

"Yes," Travis agreed. "But it doesn't seem fair that

Victoria only has peach fuzz on her head and Parker has all the curls. They're as different as night and day."

She agreed with a nod. "Where are you headed?"

"To the kitchen to get my hammer and then to the library to get Adam to help us. He can do his paperwork later. The band's going to be here by three, and we've got to be ready."

As soon as he had gone inside, Genevieve began to rock the babies. A soft warm breeze, sweet with the fragrance of wildflowers, enveloped the porch, and she stared at the mountains in the distance. She felt as though she were sitting in the middle of paradise.

She began to sing a French lullaby she remembered from childhood days, a favorite because her mother used to sing it to her every night before she tucked her into bed. The lyrics were simple and repetitive, and the melody was innocent and joyful. The lullaby brought back memories of happier, carefree days. Genevieve closed her eyes, and for a few brief, precious moments, she wasn't all alone. She was back in her childhood home, sitting in the big overstuffed chair listening to her mother sing as she pulled back the covers on her bed. The scent of lilacs enveloped Genevieve. She could hear her father's laughter floating up the stairs and feel the peace and contentment of that house. She was once again surrounded by people who loved and cherished her.

Adam stood in the doorway watching her. He was just about to push the screen door open when she began to sing, and having no wish to interrupt her, he had turned to go out the kitchen door. The music pulled him back. The rich, lustrous timbre of her voice, so pure and clear, was surely as perfect as an angel's, yet the look of tranquillity on her face was just as beautiful. The longer he listened, the more magical her voice became. Like a blade of grass drawn to the heat of the sun, he was drawn to the glorious melody. Captivated, he never wanted the song to end. He didn't make a sound, didn't move, and barely drew a breath as he let the music, and Genevieve, enchant him.

He wasn't the only man affected. One by one the crowd of men working in the yard paused to listen. Harrison was bending over to pick up his hammer when her song reached him. He straightened up and tilted his head in her direction. Travis, carrying a stack of two-by-fours across his shoulder, was halfway across the yard when he heard her singing. Like Harrison, he instinctively turned toward the porch, then went completely still and closed his eyes. Sweat dripped off his brow, the sun beat down on his face, but he was oblivious to any discomfort. In fact, he smiled with genuine pleasure.

Douglas had a nail in his mouth and a hammer in his hand and was swinging his arm in a wide arc when he heard Genevieve singing. He slowly lowered his hand and, like his brothers, turned to the sound.

The hired hands were bolder in their reaction. They dropped their tools and moved in unison to the front yard, as though they were drawn by some inexplicable force to the heavenly melody.

The babies were the only ones who weren't impressed. Both Parker and Victoria fell asleep during the first verse. Genevieve finished the lullaby and only then noticed the silence. She was given quite a start when she opened her eyes and saw the crowd watching her. One of the men began to clap, but a hard nudge and a reminder from his friend stopped the noise. However, her audience must have felt she was due some sort of appreciation, and within a few seconds every man there was smiling and tipping his hat to her.

Their grins were a bit unnerving. Embarrassed by

their attention, she gave the men a tentative smile,
looked away, and found Adam watching her. That was
even more unnerving.

He smiled. She was so astonished she smiled back.
His usual guarded expression was gone, and the look
in his eyes was one she hadn't seen before. He
looked . . . happy. He didn't seem so dangerous or
fierce to her now, yet her heart was pounding a wild
beat. The tenderness she saw in his eyes made him
even more handsome . . . and how could such a thing
be possible?

The screen door squeaked open, and he walked
over to her. She stopped rocking the babies and
simply stared up at him. He wasn't smiling any
longer, but he still looked pleased. She was feeling
flush and in dire need of a fan. She needed to get hold
of herself. She was behaving as though a man had
never looked at her before. Under his close scrutiny,
her usual confidence evaporated, and she was suddenly feeling like the shy, awkward little girl who had
made such a mess of things the first time she tried to
sing in the church choir. Fortunately, he was never
going to know how nervous he made her.

He dropped to one knee in front of her. She
couldn't imagine what he was going to do . . . and
then he reached for Parker. He was so very gentle as
he lifted the sleeping baby into his powerful arms. He
stood up, put Parker against his shoulder with one
hand splayed against the baby's back and then put his
other hand out to her.

She moved Victoria into the crook of her arm and
let Adam pull her to her feet. For several heartbeats
they simply stood staring at one another. He didn't
say a word to her, nor she to him, yet the silence
didn't seem awkward. Perhaps the babies made them
feel connected to one another for the moment.
Adam's fingers were entwined with hers, and she
didn't know if she should pull away or not.

He made the decision for her when he turned toward the door. She had to let go of him then. She assumed he was going to put Parker in his crib and wanted her to follow with Victoria.

A few minutes later, both babies were sleeping peacefully in their cribs. She was putting the blanket around Victoria when she looked up to see Adam quietly stepping out of the room.

Oh no you don't, she thought. *You aren't getting away from me this time.*

She glanced over at Parker to make certain he was covered, then picked up her skirts and rushed after Adam.

He was waiting for her on the landing. Unfortunately, she didn't know that. When she came running around the corner, she crashed into him and very nearly sent him flying over the banister. Had he been a couple of inches shorter and a few pounds lighter, she probably would have killed him, and, dear God, he never would have forgiven her then.

He buckled under the impact, let out a low grunt, and grabbed hold of her to keep her from falling down the steps.

Her sense of humor helped her get past her embarrassment. She burst into laughter in the middle of her apology.

"I didn't want you to get away before . . . I'm so sorry, Adam. I didn't mean to bump into you. Are you all right? I didn't hurt you, did I?"

He shook his head. "Are you always in such a hurry?"

His smile sent her heart racing. She stared up into his beautiful dark eyes and felt herself melting. She knew that if she didn't say or do something soon, she would find herself married to him in no time at all. Why, oh why, did he have to be such a charming man?

"I'm sorry. What did you ask?"

"Are you always in such a hurry?"

"In a hurry? No, I don't think I am."

"We need to talk, don't we, Genevieve?"

She vehemently nodded. "Yes, we need to talk."

"We'll need privacy."

As if to underline that fact, the screen door slammed shut and Cole crossed the foyer below them.

"Yes, we need privacy."

"Is something wrong?" he asked. "You seem a little nervous."

"Nervous? I seem nervous?"

He nodded. She took a deep breath and ordered herself to stop repeating his every word. The man was going to think she was a twit.

"I am a little nervous," she said. "Do you know what I think?"

He didn't have a clue. "What do you think?"

"You and I started off on the wrong foot."

"We did?"

"Yes, we did," she insisted. "It's all my fault. I shouldn't have told you I was your bride. I stunned you with my announcement, didn't I? Well, of course I did. You obviously didn't expect to find me in your bed. You looked so horrified, and you were in such a hurry to get away from me you were tripping over your own feet. I simply couldn't resist tormenting you. I didn't take offense over your conduct, but now that I think about it, I probably should have been insulted, or at the very least . . . Why are you smiling?"

He didn't tell her the truth, that he was amused by her. The play of emotions that had crossed her face as she rambled on and on was comical. She was smiling one second and glaring up at him the next. He felt like laughing, and if she hadn't been so agitated, he probably would have given in to the urge. He didn't want to hurt her feelings though. Genevieve obviously took the matter of their engagement seriously, and he was pretty certain she expected him to do the same.

It really was a hell of a mess, and he had no one but Mama Rose to blame for meddling in his private affairs. He would deal with her later, but now he needed to have a long-overdue discussion with Genevieve.

First things first. He needed to move away from her. He was standing entirely too close. Odd, but he couldn't seem to make himself step back. Her scent, so light and feminine, made him think she'd bathed in lilacs. He liked it more than he thought he should. He liked just about everything about her. He even noticed, and approved of, what she was wearing, and he had never been interested in such superficial things before. Still, the starched, high-collared white blouse and white skirt were a nice contrast to her flawless coloring. She looked as prim and proper as a banker's wife, and was as sexy as hell.

He shook himself out of his reflection. "Why don't we go down to the library."

"The library? Yes, we should go to the library."

"Good idea," he drawled out.

She inwardly groaned. She was doing it again, repeating his words. He was going to start calling her a parrot if she didn't get hold of herself and stop thinking about foolish things, such as how deep and rich the sound of his voice was and how clean and masculine his scent was. He seemed to carry the outdoors around with him.

He really had the most devastating effect on her. She let out a little sigh. "I've been dreading this."

"Dreading what?"

"Our private talk," she said. "Shall we go and get it over with?"

She sounded as though she were on her way to a firing squad. He agreed with a nod and walked by her side down the stairs. When they reached the end of the back hall, he moved forward to open the door, then stepped back so she could enter the library first.

The room was musty and smelled of old books. She found it very pleasing and looked around in fascination and approval. There were hundreds of volumes lined up on cherry wood shelves from the ceiling to the floor, and more books were piled in stacks on the hardwood floor near the windows.

The library had taken on the character of the man who occupied it, she decided. She knew from Adam's letters to his mother how much he loved to read, and she would have wagered every cent she possessed that he had already read every book there. He might even have read them more than once.

He motioned for her to take a seat. She chose one of the two overstuffed leather chairs facing the desk, sat down on the very edge of the seat, with her knees and her ankles pressed together and her back as straight as a ruler, and folded her hands in her lap.

She couldn't sit still long. While he was getting comfortable in his chair behind the desk, she nervously began to tap her heels against the floor. She stared down at her lap so she could concentrate, and rehearsed what she would say to him.

She thought it would be better if she let him speak first, and after he was finished, she would then gently—yes, gently—explain that her circumstances had changed and she couldn't marry him. She would be as diplomatic as a statesman so that she wouldn't injure his feelings or damage his pride.

Adam sat back in his chair and stared at her, patiently waiting for her to tell him what was on her mind. After several minutes passed in silence, he decided it was up to him to begin. He knew exactly what he wanted to say to her, for he'd been thinking about it all week long. Why then was it so difficult for him to get started?

He cleared his throat. The tapping got faster and louder.

"Genevieve, I'm not certain what your understanding with Mama Rose was, but I—"

She jumped to her feet. "Oh, Adam, I can't do it. I just can't."

"You can't what?"

"I can't marry you. I wish I could, but I can't. I wanted to explain right away, but you've been avoiding me all week long, which makes me think you don't really want to marry me anyway, and this personal matter wasn't something I wanted to talk about in front of your relatives. It's all so awkward, isn't it? Your mother put both of us in such a peculiar position. Are we engaged or aren't we? No, of course we aren't. Will it surprise you to know that I do want to marry you, or at least I used to want to marry you? For heaven's sake, don't look so surprised. I'm telling you the truth. Everything's changed though, and I can't possibly marry you now. No, it's out of the question, and even if you did want to marry me, well, eventually you'd find out about the trouble I'm in, and then you'd be horrified you ever entertained the notion. Do you see? I'm saving you from making a terrible mistake. I'm so sorry to disappoint you. Truly I am. You're just going to have to get over me. Broken hearts do mend. There, I've had my say. We can't get married, no matter how much you want to, and I apologize for deliberately misleading you. It was insensitive and cruel of me."

She finally paused long enough to take a breath. She knew she'd made a mess out of her explanation, and even while she had been rambling on and on, she'd kept telling herself to stop, but she couldn't seem to make herself do it. He probably thought she was crazy. His expression didn't give her a hint of what he was thinking, and she could only conclude that he was too stunned to react at all. Some of the words she'd blurted out kept repeating inside her head. Dear God, she'd started out telling him she didn't believe he wanted to marry her, and by the time she'd finished, she was insisting that his broken heart would mend. Oh, yes, he had to think she was demented. Mortified, she turned her attention to the wall behind him, pretending great interest in the framed map hanging there.

"I have to 'get over' you?"

She was relieved there wasn't any laughter in his voice when he asked the question. She gave him a weak nod and said, "Yes, you do."

"I see. You said you misled me. When exactly did you do that?"

She continued to stand and stare at the map while she answered him. "The night we met, I introduced myself as your bride. That was a falsehood."

"Ah, yes, I remember."

She dared a quick look at him. The warmth in his eyes had a strangely calming effect on her, and she began to relax.

"Are you always so self-assured?"

He laughed. "No."

"I think maybe you are. You don't get riled easily, do you?"

"No, I don't. Did you want to rile me?"

"No, of course not. You really do have an odd effect on me. I'm very relaxed around your family, but you . . ."

"I what?"

She shrugged and then decided to change the subject. "Your mother didn't tell me what a nice-looking man you were. It doesn't change anything. I still can't marry you, and I wouldn't marry any man just because he was handsome. I've learned from experience that appearances are misleading."

"Mama Rose didn't tell me how pretty you were. Why don't you sit down and tell me about the trouble you're in. Maybe I can help."

"Trouble? Why do you think I'm in trouble?"

Her voice rose an octave, and she seemed astonished that he would ask her such a question. He held on to his patience. "You just told me you were."

She didn't remember. "I spoke out of turn. I was in such a hurry to get everything said, and I was very nervous. I'm sure you must have noticed. I was talking a mile a minute, but I so wanted you to understand. And I was concerned about hurting your feelings. I didn't, did I?"

"Hurt my feelings? No, you didn't," he assured her with a smile he couldn't quite contain. "I might be able to help you, Genevieve, if you'll tell me what the problem is," he insisted once again.

She shook her head. She didn't want to lie to him, but she didn't want to tell him the truth either, for then he would be involved and could very well end up in trouble too.

"I don't have a problem."

She didn't think she could have been more emphatic, yet from his frown, she knew he still wasn't convinced. Once again she tried to get him to talk about something else.

She nodded toward the wall behind him. "Your mother showed me that map right after she purchased it for you. Why did you frame it and hang it on your wall? That wasn't what she wanted you to do with it. You were supposed to take it with you when you set out to see the world."

He knew she was deliberately evading his question, and that only made him more curious to find out what was troubling her. He wasn't usually intrusive, but she was a guest in his house and a close friend of his mother's, and if she really was in trouble, then he should try to help. He couldn't imagine that she was involved in anything serious though. She was such a sweet, innocent woman, one who undoubtedly had been sheltered by her family. What possible trouble could she have gotten into?

His mind leapt from one possibility to another. "Did you leave a suitor pining after you when you left New Orleans?"

The question gave her pause. "No," she answered. "I wasn't in New Orleans long enough to meet anyone. Why would you ask me such a question?"

"I was just curious."

"Are you always this curious with all your guests?"

"Only the ones I find myself engaged to," he teased.

She hastened to correct him. "You were engaged, Adam, but you aren't any longer."

He laughed again. "That's right," he agreed. "How long were you in New Orleans?"

"Two weeks."

"Just long enough to see the sights?"

"I wasn't there to see the sights. I was singing in a choir, but then I decided it was time for me to leave. Now it's your turn. Answer my question and tell me why you haven't left here to travel the world. I know you wanted to, because I read all the letters you wrote to Mama Rose."

He raised an eyebrow in reaction. "You did? Why would you—"

She wouldn't let him finish. "I love Mama Rose, and I wanted to know everything I could about her family. It was something I could share with her. We met at church," she added. "Then I joined the choir and traveled from place to place."

"You have a beautiful voice. Did you ever think about teaching music?"

"No, but I did think about a career on the stage. Then I came to my senses. I sing in church, and I occasionally sing to babies," she said with a smile.

"Now it's your turn to answer a question. Tell me, why haven't you gone out to see the world?"

"I can see the world every time I turn my head and look at a map, and I can go from port to port by simply opening one of my books and reading."

"It isn't at all the same. You've become too complacent, Adam. Think of all the adventures you could have. What happened to your dream? You've forgotten about it, haven't you? Your mother didn't forget, and that's why she gave you the map. She showed me all the presents she was bringing to her sons and her daughter, and every one of them had special significance. Mary Rose continues the family tradition by wearing her mother's brooch, and Douglas carries his gold watch with him. Travis told me he takes his books everywhere he goes. Why, just last night he was rereading *The Republic*. I haven't seen Cole's compass yet," she added.

Before she could continue, Adam interjected, "He hasn't seen it yet either."

She looked perplexed. "I don't understand. Why hasn't he seen it? Didn't Mama Rose give it to him?"

"Both the compass and the gold carrying case were either stolen or borrowed from Mama Rose."

"Which was it, for heaven's sake? Stolen or borrowed?"

"It depends on who you ask. Cole insists it was stolen, but the rest of us think it was borrowed. I'll admit that when Mama Rose first told us what happened, we all thought it was stolen, but since then ;most of us have changed our minds."

"Tell me what happened," she insisted. She sat down, folded her hands together, and waited for him to begin.

"Mama Rose was waiting for a train at one of the stations on her way here. She showed the compass and the gold case to a man who was traveling with her. He was also headed for Montana," he continued. "According to Mama Rose, the two of them became friends and confided in one another."

"Your mother's a good judge of character."

"Yes, she is," he agreed. "She told us that he looked out for her on the journey and was very kind to her."

"He gained her confidence, and after a while, she began to trust him," she said with a nod that suggested she understood what had happened.

"Yes, she trusted him."

Her voice was edged with sadness when she said, "I bet I know what happened then. He betrayed her, didn't he?"

Adam found her reaction to the story intriguing. He had expected her to be a little curious, but she seemed upset about it.

"Cole thinks he did betray her," he said. "Is that what happened to you, Genevieve? Did you trust someone who betrayed you?"

The question startled her. She quickly shook her head in denial. "We're talking about your mother, not me."

"Are we?"

"Yes," she insisted. "I do find the story disturbing," she admitted. "Has anyone notified the authorities about the theft? They might be able to get the compass back."

"So you think he stole the compass?"

"Yes, I do. The gold case is very valuable. I'm telling you, Adam, you just can't trust anyone these days."

He was trying not to smile. She had formed her conclusion without knowing half the facts. She and Cole had a lot in common. Like his brother, Genevieve was willing to think the worst.

"You sound as cynical as Cole."

"I am cynical," she said. "I'll bet the authorities

also think the compass was stolen. What did they have to say?"

"It's complicated."

"Why?"

"The man who has the compass *is* the authority."

Her hand flew to her throat. "What's this?" she demanded.

"A U.S. marshal has the compass. His name is Daniel Ryan."

She was astounded. "The thief's a marshal? How shameful. Your dear mother must be devastated."

"No, she isn't devastated at all. She's convinced herself that he never meant to keep the compass. There was a crowd trying to get on the train, and she and Ryan were separated. He just happened to be holding the compass and the gold case at the time. She believes he'll bring Cole's gift here as soon as he finishes his more pressing business. Cole thinks Mama Rose is being very naive. From the description we have of Ryan, it does seem peculiar to all of us that he could be pushed around in a crowd. He's a big man with muscle."

"Is he as big as you are?"

Adam shrugged. "If the description's accurate, then yes, he is."

She mulled the story over in her mind for a moment and then condemned Ryan. "He stole it all right."

"Then you also believe Mama Rose is being naive?"

Genevieve stood up and began to pace around the room. "She has to have faith in Daniel Ryan, and you should let her."

"Why?" he asked.

"Because otherwise she would have to accept that she had been duped, and that's very difficult for anyone to admit. She would feel foolish and stupid, and blame herself. Yes, she would. She wouldn't be able to sleep worrying about it."

She turned at the window to look at him and knew by his expression that her outburst had been a bit extreme. She took a deep breath and tried to explain herself. "You must think it strange that I would become so passionate on your mother's behalf. It's just that she's such a good-hearted woman and it wounds me to think that anyone would take advantage of her. I wouldn't advise going after Daniel Ryan though, because it will only make matters worse."

"Why would it make matters worse?"

"Because in the end, it would be his word against hers."

"And you think that because he's a marshal, the law would be on his side?"

"Yes, of course," she replied. "It's naive to think otherwise. Ryan holds a position of power and influence over others, and if Mama Rose doesn't use her wits to figure a way to outsmart him, then all will be lost."

Adam stood up and came around the desk. "Tell me something. Did you use your wits to outsmart . . ."

He stopped in the middle of his question when Genevieve headed for the door.

"Don't run away. I'll stop prying into your personal life. I promise."

Her hand was on the doorknob, and he could tell from her frown that she didn't believe him.

"Your affairs are none of my business," he insisted. "I just thought I might be able to help."

"I don't need your help."

He leaned against the desk, folded his arms across his chest, and nodded. "Obviously not."

She took a step toward him. "It was very kind of you to offer. Please don't think I'm not grateful."

"I don't."

She visibly relaxed and moved closer.

"You smell like lilacs. I like it," he said.

She smiled. "Thank you," she said. "And thank you also for offering to help. It was very kind of you, but since I don't happen to have a problem, I don't need your assistance."

She wasn't a good liar. She couldn't quite look him in the eyes when she insisted she wasn't in trouble. He wouldn't challenge her though. He knew she'd head for the door again if he didn't agree with her.

"No," he said. "You don't have a problem, and you don't need help."

"That's right."

"Mama Rose doesn't need help either. She made all of us promise not to go after Ryan, but now that we know where he is, Cole's having a real hard time keeping his word."

"Where is the marshal?"

"About a hundred miles from here, in Crawford," he answered. "He lives in Texas, but he's working out of the office there while he rounds up a gang hiding out in the hills. Word has it, he's determined to take them back to Texas to stand trial."

"Couldn't one of you go to Crawford and have a little talk with him? I'm sure he'd give you the compass once he knows who you are."

Adam shook his head. "We have to wait until he brings it here because we promised we would. I figure he'll get around to it one of these days. Besides, the circumstances changed, and Cole's the only one who still wants to go after him."

"How did the circumstances change?"

"Ryan saved Travis's life."

She was astonished. "Tell me what happened."

He told her the story of Travis's encounter with the O'Toole brothers. "They ambushed him, shot him in the back. If Ryan hadn't gotten there when he did, Travis would never have made it."

"I wish you had mentioned this earlier," she said. "I have to revise my opinion now. Why, he probably didn't steal the compass at all. The man proved that he's honorable by coming to Travis's rescue. Shame on you, Adam, for making him out to be guilty."

The sparkle in her eyes told him she was teasing. She really was a beautiful woman, and that smile of hers was doing crazy things to his heartbeat. He found himself wondering what she would feel like in his arms. If he kissed her the way he wanted to, he knew he'd shock her sensibilities, but that didn't stop him from thinking about it.

"You made him out to be guilty."

Her remark jarred him out of his daydream. "I what?"

She repeated her statement. He shook his head. "I did no such thing. You drew your own conclusions before I could give you all the details."

She burst out laughing. "I got all riled up for nothing. I won't worry about Mama Rose any longer. I've taken up too much of your time. You're needed outside," she reminded him. She glanced back at the map once again. "You should take the map out of the frame. Your mother doesn't want you to give up on your dreams, and neither do I. You should see all the wonderful places you've read about before it's too late, and if you ever find your way to Paris, be sure to look me up."

She turned to leave. He didn't know what compelled him to do it, but he grabbed hold of her hand and pulled her back.

"You're going to France?"

"Yes. My grandfather lives there, and he's all the family I have left now."

"When will you leave?"

"In a couple of days."

The news that she would be going so far away bothered him, and he couldn't understand why. He should be happy to be rid of her, shouldn't he? And now that he thought about it, why hadn't he been elated when she'd told him she couldn't marry him? He had intended to say those very words to her.

Adam knew he wasn't making any sense, and that made him angry. He immediately let go of her hand and watched her walk away.

Then he got up and went back to work. His involvement with Genevieve Perry was over.

Three

It had only just begun.

Quite a crowd attended the party, and everyone seemed to be having a good time. Adam and Cole stood near the bandstand watching the couples dance to the gyrating, foot-stomping sounds of Billie Bob and Joe Boy's Band. Isabelle and Douglas came twirling past, and right behind them were Travis and his wife, Emily. If their laughter was any indication, the four of them were thoroughly enjoying themselves. Mama Rose was delighted by all the commotion. She sat at one of the picnic tables, flanked by Dooley and Ghost, two family friends, and all three of them, Adam noticed, kept time to the music by clapping their hands and tapping their feet.

Cole nudged his brother in his side. "Isn't that Clarence riding down the hill?"

Adam squinted toward the mountain. "It looks like him."

"We invited him, but he turned us down because he had to work the telegraph office. Someone has to be on duty all the time. Maybe he's bringing a wire to someone."

"Maybe he got someone else to work for him," Adam suggested.

Douglas and Isabelle came dancing past again. Cole waved to them and then said, "I never thought Travis or Douglas would ever get married, and now look at them."

"They're happy and they found good women. What about you, Cole? Do you think you'll ever get married?"

"No," he replied, his voice emphatic. "I'm not cut out for marriage. You are though. What happened with Genevieve? Did you have your talk with her?"

"Yes."

"I hope you let her down easy. She's a real sweetheart, and I'd hate to see her get hurt."

Adam shook his head. "If you're worried about her feelings, don't be. You've got it all backwards. She talked to me. She doesn't want to marry me either."

"Why the hell not?"

"Her circumstances have changed," Adam said. "Besides, we were never really engaged. That was just Mama Rose's dream. She's hell-bent on getting all of us married."

"You must have been happy Genevieve let you off the hook."

Adam shrugged. He thought about lying to his brother and then changed his mind. Cole would see right through him, and if anyone would understand, he would.

"I wasn't happy or relieved. My reaction was kind of strange."

"How's that?"

He looked at his brother when he answered. "I got mad."

Cole shook his head. "You really got mad?"

"I just said I did. Genevieve didn't know it though."

"That doesn't make any sense at all. You've been avoiding the woman all week long, and now you're telling me you want to marry her?"

"No, that isn't what I'm telling you."

"Then why did you get mad?"

Adam let out a weary sigh. "I don't know."

Cole let the matter go. "Are you going to dance with her?"

"I hadn't thought about it. I don't even know where she is."

Cole motioned toward the porch. Mary Rose and Genevieve were carrying pies out to add to the dessert table. Both women had on white aprons over their dresses. Mary Rose was wearing her new store-bought blue skirt and blouse, and Genevieve was dressed in pale pink. Standing side by side, they were a handsome pair.

Adam couldn't take his gaze off of Genevieve. She was smiling over something Mary Rose had just said to her.

"Genevieve sure is pretty, isn't she?" Cole remarked.

"Yeah, she's pretty."

"She's tall."

"You think so?"

Adam turned around to watch the band. Cole didn't take the hint. "Mary Rose has to look up at her."

"So what? Our sister has to look up at everybody."

"You don't have to get defensive. I'm not finding fault with Genevieve. I like tall women. Have you noticed how shapely she is?"

"Of course I noticed. What's your game, Cole? Are you trying to make me angry?"

"No, I'm trying to get you to realize women like Genevieve don't come along very often. She sure is sweet."

"Then you marry her," he snapped.

Cole laughed. "You want her, don't you?"

"Damn it, Cole . . ."

"All right," his brother said. "I won't hound you any longer."

Adam started to walk away, but Cole's next remark pulled him back.

"It looks like Clarence is headed for the house."

"Maybe he needs to talk to Harrison," Adam suggested as he watched their brother-in-law step forward to shake Clarence's hand.

"Guess again," Cole said when Clarence turned to Genevieve and tried to hand an envelope to her. She gave the pie she was holding to Harrison, wiped her hands on her apron, and then accepted the wire.

"It's got to be bad news," Cole said.

"Maybe not," Adam said, and even he realized how unconvinced he sounded.

"No one ever sends good news in a wire. It costs too much. It's bad all right. Someone must have died. You ought to go comfort her."

"You go."

"I wasn't engaged to her; you were."

"For God's sake, there wasn't any engagement."

When Clarence turned to go down the steps, Adam saw his expression clearly.

"Clarence looks scared."

Cole nodded. "He sure is in a hurry to leave, isn't he?"

Adam turned back to Genevieve. "Why doesn't she open the envelope? What's she waiting for?"

"Maybe she wants to stare at it a little longer while she gets her courage up. No one's ever eager to get bad news."

"We shouldn't be watching her."

"Why not?" Cole asked.

"It's intrusive. She probably wants privacy."

He watched her tuck the unopened envelope into the pocket of her apron before taking the pie back from Harrison and hurrying down the steps. She put the dessert on the table with the other baked goods, then turned around and walked away from the crowd.

Adam forced himself to turn to the couples twirling about the dance floor, but he kept glancing back at Genevieve.

He saw her stop when she reached the far side of the corral near the barn. She pulled the envelope out, tore it open, and read the contents.

The news couldn't have been good. Even with the distance separating them, Adam could see how shaken she was. She couldn't stand up straight. She staggered back against the fence and turned away from him, but not before he saw the fear on her face.

"Maybe you ought to go find out what the trouble is," Cole suggested.

Adam shook his head. "She obviously wants to be alone. If she tells us what the news was and we can help, then we will. Quit giving me that look, Cole. I'm not going to intrude into her personal life again, and neither are you."

"Again? What are you talking about?"

"Never mind."

Isabelle was suddenly standing in front of Adam, demanding that he dance with her. Emily grabbed hold of Cole's hand at the same time and pulled him onto the dance floor.

Adam tried to keep track of Genevieve. He saw her crumple up the wire and put it back in her apron, but then the music started and he lost her in the crowd.

After the dance ended, he went searching for her. Harrison intercepted him to tell him that Mama Rose was about to open her presents. Since the family was giving her a trip to Scotland, Harrison thought it would be a nice touch if he played the bagpipes. Adam couldn't talk him out of it. He joined his sister and his brothers on the side of the bandstand and tried to appear interested. He nudged Cole and asked him in a low voice if he'd seen Genevieve.

Cole shook his head. He was going to suggest that she was probably inside the house, but then Harrison began to play, and the piercing noise was so deafening, he knew Adam wouldn't hear him.

"He's getting better, isn't he?" Mary Rose shouted.

"No," all four brothers shouted back.

Their sister wasn't offended. She maintained her smile for her husband's benefit and gave Douglas a hard shove when he put his hands over his wife's ears.

Genevieve was standing in the center of the crowd on the opposite side of the bandstand, watching the Clayborne family—the four brothers side by side, Emily and Isabelle leaning back against their husbands. Their expressions were comical, but she thought Adam's was the most revealing. Like his brothers and his sister, he was smiling, yet every time Harrison tried to hit a high note and missed, Adam would visibly flinch.

They were all such good-hearted people and so very loyal to one another. They were united now in giving Harrison their encouragement and support, and though it was apparent from their forced smiles that they thought the music was terrible, she knew they would cheer him when he was finished and never admit to any outsider that the sound had been less than perfect. And that was what family was all about.

God, how she envied all of them. She longed to walk across the dance floor and stand in front of

Adam and lean back against him. She wanted to belong to his family, but most of all, she wanted to be loved by him.

It was a fool's dream, she told herself. She whispered a good-bye in Mama Rose's direction, and then turned and walked away.

Four

The party didn't wind down until after midnight. Riders with fiery torches lighted the way back to Blue Belle for those guests who lived in the nearby town and wanted to go home. The guests from Hammond stayed overnight. They slept on cots in the parlor and the dining room, filled the bunkhouse, and spilled out onto the porch. Cole gave up his bed to the Cohens, and Adam let old man Corbett sleep in the bunk bed he'd used all week. The brothers weren't inconvenienced, for they much preferred sleeping outside under the stars, away from the crowd.

Adam left at dawn the following morning with three hired hands to round up the mustangs grazing on sweet grass down in Maple Valley, and he didn't return to Rosehill until late that afternoon.

Cole was waiting for him on the front porch. He handed Adam a beer and sat down on the top step.

He didn't waste time getting to the news. "Genevieve's gone."

Adam didn't show any outward reaction. He took

44

his hat off, tossed it onto a nearby chair, and sat down next to his brother. He took a long swallow of his drink and remarked that it was damned hot today.

"You look tired," Cole remarked.

"I am tired," Adam replied. "Have all the guests gone home?"

"Yes, the last of them left around noon."

"When are you leaving for Texas to bring the cattle up?"

"Tomorrow."

Several minutes passed in silence. Adam stared at the distant mountains and tried to ignore the unease he felt about Genevieve. As soon as Cole had given him the news, his gut and his throat both tightened up on him. Why had she left so abruptly, and why hadn't she told him good-bye? Maybe he shouldn't have hounded her with questions, but damn it, she'd let it slip that she was in trouble, and he had naturally wanted to find out the particulars so that he could help. No, he decided. His few questions wouldn't have made her so skittish that she would pack up and leave.

The telegram had to be the reason she'd taken off. He remembered the fear he'd seen on her face after she'd read the wire. He should have gone to her then and demanded that she confide in him.

He let out a loud sigh. He knew then what he was going to have to do and was already getting angry about it.

"Hell," he muttered.

"What?"

"Nothing. Did Genevieve say good-bye to anyone?"

"No, she didn't tell anyone she was leaving. She just took off. Mama Rose is up in arms about it. She says it isn't like Genevieve to leave without saying her thank-yous. She says she's a well-bred young lady with impeccable manners. I think Genevieve was spooked by that telegram," Cole added. "But Mama Rose thinks you chased her away."

Adam rolled his eyes heavenward. "Genevieve must have left with some of the guests last night. She's too smart to go off on her own."

"Maybe so," Cole allowed. "It's odd though. She was supposed to ride with the Emersons to Salt Lake, and they aren't leaving town until tomorrow."

"Maybe they decided to leave earlier."

"In the dark? They're old, not crazy. Besides, they were here last night."

Adam's unease intensified. Had she gone off on her own? The possibility sent chills down his spine. No, she wouldn't have done that. She was too intelligent to do such a rash, irresponsible thing. She would surely be aware of the danger a woman alone would face in the wild. Women were hard to come by in some of the more remote areas, and pretty women like Genevieve were considered prizes for the taking by some of the less civilized mountain clans.

Cole was watching his brother closely. "You don't seem too broken up over her leaving," he remarked.

Adam shrugged indifference. "It's her life. She can do whatever she wants."

"What if she took off on her own?"

"There isn't anything I can do about that."

Cole smiled. "It isn't working, Adam."

"What isn't working?"

"Your I-don't-give-a-damn attitude. You're trying to act like you aren't worried about her, and we both know you are."

His brother didn't deny it. "I wish I knew what was in that telegram. Whatever it was scared her. Maybe someone close to her got sick. That would scare a woman, wouldn't it?"

"That would scare a man too," Cole said. "You don't think she's in any kind of trouble, do you?"

"It can't be anything serious. I was pretty sure that

there was something wrong, but she denied it. She looked me right in the eye and told me she didn't need any help. She said it was just a minor inconvenience."

"You think she was telling you the truth?"

"About her problem being a minor one? Yeah, I do. She's led a real sheltered life, and I can't imagine she has any real serious problems."

"I think Genevieve's real smart, but even smart people do crazy things when they're scared."

"Such as?"

"Riding out at night all alone."

Adam refused to believe that she would take such a chance. "I'm sure she got a ride with someone."

Cole didn't argue with him. "Maybe you ought to go into town and have a little talk with Clarence. You can be real intimidating when you want to, and I'll bet you could get him to tell you what was in that wire."

"If he tells me, he'll lose his job. Wires are supposed to be kept confidential."

"So?"

Adam shook his head. "Clarence is too ethical." He spat the words out as though they were foul. He stood up, grabbed his hat, and headed for the door. "I've wasted enough time."

"Where are you going?"

"Back to work as soon as I change my shirt. I'm going to be up half the night catching up on all the paperwork, and tomorrow I've got to start breaking in the mustangs so we can sell them at the auction next month, and I—"

"You're going after her, aren't you?"

Adam gave his brother a look that suggested he wanted to punch him for asking such a stupid question. "What do you think?"

He didn't stay outside long enough to hear Cole's answer. He went upstairs to his room, stripped out of his shirt, and washed the dirt and grime off. He could have sworn the scent of lilacs was on the towel he used, but that was the only reminder that Genevieve had occupied his room.

Her suitcase was gone from the corner. There was an empty space in the wardrobe where her clothes had hung, and the jewelry and hair clips he'd noticed on the dresser yesterday when he'd come in to get clean clothes were also gone.

She hadn't left anything behind. Yet the memory of her smile lingered in his mind, and he knew it was going to take him a long while to forget her.

He decided to get busy. He went downstairs to grab something to eat before he tackled the paperwork. Mary Rose was sitting at the kitchen table with a pen and paper in her hands. She smiled when she saw him.

"You're back early. Are you hungry? I made soup, but it isn't as good as Mama Rose's."

"I thought you went home," he said.

"We're leaving in a few minutes. I wanted to copy down this recipe first. Sit down and I'll get you a bowl. You are going to try my soup, aren't you?"

"Sure," he said.

She stood up and reached for the apron she'd draped over the back of her chair. Adam had only just taken his seat when he bounded back to his feet.

"The apron," he announced.

She slipped the garment over her head and then looked down to see if something was wrong with it.

"It looks fine to me."

"Not yours," he said, his impatience evident in his brisk tone. "The apron Genevieve was wearing. Was it hers?" he asked, wondering if women packed such things when they traveled.

"No, I loaned her one of Mama Rose's. I didn't want her to get her dress—"

Adam cut her off. "Did she give it back?"

"For heaven's sake, of course she gave it back. What's the matter with you?"

"Nothing's the matter. Where is it?"

"The apron?"

"Yes, damn it, the apron. Where is it?"

Her eyes widened in reaction to his bizarre behavior. It wasn't like Adam to ever lose his temper, but he appeared to be on the verge of doing just that. He was usually so calm and in control. Nothing ever riled him.

"Why are you getting so upset about an apron?" she demanded.

"I'm not upset. Now answer me. Where is it?"

She gave him a frown to let him know she didn't appreciate his surly attitude.

"I suppose it's hanging with the others on the hooks in the pantry."

Adam was already halfway across the kitchen before his sister had finished explaining. She followed him to the doorway and stood there watching him sort through the clutter of coats and hats and scarves and bibs, tossing them every which way until most of them were on the floor behind him.

"You're picking all those up," she said. "Adam, what's come over you?"

"Where the hell is it?"

"It's the white one on your left with the two lace pockets," she said. "Why do you want it?"

Adam lifted the apron from the hook and quickly searched the pockets. He felt like shouting with victory when he pulled out the crumpled piece of paper. Just as he had hoped, in her haste to leave, Genevieve had forgotten the wire.

He unfolded the paper, moved into the light, and read the message.

Then he exploded. "Son of a bitch."

"Watch your language," Mary Rose demanded. She moved close to her brother's side and tried to see what he was holding.

She wasn't quick enough. He had already refolded the paper before she could see anything.

"What is it?"

"A telegram."

"That's Genevieve's," she said. "I was standing next to her when Clarence gave the wire to her. Shame on you, Adam. You shouldn't have read it. It's confidential."

Cole came up behind his sister in time to hear her protest and offered his opinion.

"Sure he should read it. Who's it from, Adam?"

"A woman named Lottie."

Adam finally looked at him. Cole could tell from the look in his brother's eyes that it was serious. Mary Rose didn't seem to notice, however.

"I know what it says," she announced.

Adam turned to her. "You do?"

"Yes."

"And you didn't tell anyone?"

"Don't yell at me," she snapped. "Genevieve told me her friend was expecting a baby and promised to have her husband send a wire to let her know if she had a boy or a girl."

"Is that so?" Adam asked.

Mary Rose nodded. "She had a girl," she said. "I can't understand why you would get so upset over someone else's personal . . ."

She stopped talking when Cole put his hands on her shoulders and suggested she take a good look at Adam's expression.

Their brother looked furious. "How bad is it?" Cole asked him.

In answer, Adam handed the wire to him. Cole unfolded the paper and read the message out loud.

"Run for your life. They know where you are. They're coming for you."

"Good Lord," Mary Rose cried out.

Cole whistled at the same time. "Son of a . . ."

"How could anyone want to harm such a sweet, loving young lady?" Mary Rose asked.

"I thought you told me she wasn't in trouble," Cole said.

"That's what she told me," Adam muttered.

"She lied."

"No kidding. Of course she lied."

Mary Rose shook her head. "She must have had a good reason not to involve us."

"We are involved if trouble is coming here," Cole replied.

"I thought we had become good friends over the past week. She acted as though she didn't have a care in the world. Are you going to go after her, Adam?"

"Hell, yes."

"Mama Rose is going to be beside herself with worry when she hears about this."

Adam gave his sister a hard look. "She isn't going to hear about it. There isn't any reason to worry her."

Mary Rose agreed with a quick nod. "Yes, you're right. I won't tell her."

Adam started for the door, but Mary Rose grabbed hold of his hand to detain him.

"Why are you so angry?"

"It's a hell of an inconvenience to drop everything and go chasing after her, and I don't much like knowing trouble's coming to Rosehill. Cole, you're going to have to put off your trip to Texas for another week or two and stay around here."

"I will," he assured his brother.

"If anyone comes looking for Genevieve—"

"I'll know what to do."

Adam left Rosehill fifteen minutes later. Genevieve Perry was about to find out what real trouble was.

Five

Genevieve was trying hard not to be afraid and failing miserably. She sat in front of her campfire with her legs tucked underneath her, gripping a gun in one hand and a heavy tree branch in the other. There weren't any stars out tonight, and it was so dark she couldn't see beyond the circle of the fire. She had never been bothered by the dark before, not even as a child, but then she'd always lived inside a nice strong house in the heart of the city with locks on every door and a mother and father to look after her. Now she was all alone and sitting in the middle of the forest, where all sorts of wild animals roamed about looking for food. She couldn't see the predators, but she knew they were there because she could hear them, and that made the dark all the more terrifying.

At night, the forest shrieked with life. Every sound was magnified. A twig snapped nearby and she flinched, her heart pounding frantically. She was certain an animal had made the noise, and she began to fervently pray it wasn't anything bigger or more dangerous than a rabbit. God only knew what she would do if a mountain lion or a bear wandered into her camp. The idea of becoming some animal's next meal didn't sit well with her, and she began to imagine all sorts of horrible ways she would die.

She began to hum one of her favorite hymns to take her mind off her dark thoughts until she realized the hymn was about death and redemption. Then she stopped and sagged against the tree behind her. She slowly stretched her legs out, crossed one ankle over the other, and willed herself to stop having such crazy thoughts. She would get through this night the same way she'd gotten through the past two. She would keep her eyes open and her wits sharp. Sleep was out of the question.

She never heard Adam coming. One second she was all alone, and the next he was sitting beside her and had her gun in his hand.

She was so startled to see him she screamed. She jumped back, struck her head against the tree, and cried out again. Her heart felt as though it had just leapt into her throat. How in heaven's name had he managed to drop down beside her without making any noise? As soon as she could find her voice, she would ask him that very question.

He didn't say a word to her. She watched him drop the gun on the ground between them. She stared stupidly at the weapon for several seconds before she turned to look up at him.

She had never been so happy to see anyone in all her life. He didn't look happy to see her though. His anger was more than apparent in the darkening of his eyes and the set of his jaw.

She wanted to hug him. She frowned instead and put her hand over her heart. "Adam, you scared me."

He didn't have anything to say about that. She took another breath and then admitted, "I didn't hear you coming."

"You weren't supposed to hear me."

They stared into each other's eyes for what seemed an eternity without saying another word. He was trying to calm his temper and kept telling himself that he had gotten to her in time, that nothing god-awful had happened to her, and that she was all right—for the moment. Relief intensified his anger, and, honest to God, he wanted to kiss her and shake some sense into her at the same time. He didn't give in to either inclination.

She was so thankful not to be alone any longer, tears welled up in her eyes.

He saw them. "What are you doing out here?"

"I'm camping. What are you doing here?"

"I came to get you."

Her eyes widened. "You did? Why?"

He didn't explain but asked another question instead. "Why did you leave the ranch so abruptly?"

She turned away and stared at the fire. "I felt it was time for me to leave."

"What kind of answer is that?" he demanded.

"Lower your voice," she whispered.

"Why?"

"I don't want to . . . The animals will . . ."

"What about the animals?"

"If they hear us, they'll know we're here and they might come into camp."

He tried not to smile. "Animals are also directed by scent."

"I heard a mountain lion a little while ago."

"He won't bother you."

"You're sure?"

"Yes."

She visibly relaxed and leaned into his side. Her arm rubbed against his when she turned to him again. "There aren't any stars out tonight."

"Why did you leave in the middle of the night

without telling anyone good-bye? Why were you in such a hurry?"

He already knew the answer, but he was curious to find out if she would tell him the truth. If she did, it would be a novelty, he decided. His frown darkened as he thought about what an adroit liar she was.

His scowl was hot enough to set her hair on fire. Her spine stiffened in reaction. "I know you're angry, but—"

He cut her off. "Hell, yes. I'm angry."

"Why?"

He shook his head at her. "Don't you realize what could have happened to you? A beautiful woman like you can't go riding off in the wild without escorts. Do you have some sort of a death wish, Genevieve? Is that it? I know you're smart, but honest to God, I can't figure out why you would do such a foolish thing. Don't you care about the danger you're in?"

"I'm perfectly capable of taking care of myself, and if you came all this way just to give me a piece of your mind, then it was a wasted trip. Go back home."

She had tried to sound as angry as he had, but she was so rattled at the moment she didn't know if she'd accomplished the feat or not. He thought she was beautiful. The comment, made so matter-of-factly in the middle of his blistering lecture, took her by complete surprise. No one had ever called her beautiful before, and she had certainly never thought of herself that way. She was built all wrong. She was too tall, too thin, and her hair was too short. Yet Adam thought she was beautiful.

He couldn't figure out what had just come over her. She was staring off into space, a dreamy expression in her eyes. A hint of a smile crossed her face, and if he hadn't known better, he would have thought she was daydreaming.

He heard her sigh. It was long and drawn out, the

kind of sigh a woman makes after she's been satisfied. Ah, hell, he thought to himself. Now wasn't the time to be thinking about such things.

"You were about to tell me why you left the ranch in the middle of the night without a word," he reminded her in a voice that sounded like a bear growling.

The reminder jarred her out of the fantasy she was having about living happily ever after.

"It wasn't the middle of the night. It was evening, and I wanted to say good-bye, honestly I did, but I was in a hurry and there wasn't time."

"Obviously not," he said. "Do you want to tell me why you were in such a hurry?"

"No."

Her abrupt answer didn't please him. He held his patience and said, "You left something behind."

"I did? What did I leave?"

"The telegram."

She closed her eyes. "You read it, didn't you?"

"Oh, yes, I read it."

She heard a faint rustling and gripped the branch with both hands as she squinted into the darkness. "I think something's out there. Did you hear that noise just now?"

"It's just the wind kicking up the leaves."

"I'm not so sure," she whispered.

"I am," he insisted. "You haven't done a lot of camping, have you, Genevieve?" His exasperation was obvious.

"No, I haven't. It's an adventure for me."

"You're trembling."

"It's chilly tonight. I will admit I was a little nervous before you arrived. I'm not nervous now. I'm glad you're here, Adam, even though you're angry with me."

"There's a town less than five miles from here. The Garrisons are a real nice couple who live on the outskirts. They rent out rooms. If you had asked—"

"I can't afford to spend any more money," she interrupted. "The trip to Rosehill cost more than I had anticipated. Besides, it wouldn't have been an adventure if I took a room for the night. I'm experiencing life. I'm not content to read about it the way you are."

He ignored her barb. "You could probably put that branch down now. What were you planning to do with it?"

She tossed it aside before she answered him. "I was going to swat animals away with it."

He didn't laugh at her, but the look he gave her suggested he thought she had lost her mind. She lifted her shoulders. "It seemed like a good idea at the time."

"You have a gun," he reminded her.

"I know I have a gun. I hoped I wouldn't have to use it. I'm the intruder here, not the wild animals. This is their home."

"Have you ever fired a gun before?"

"No."

Her answer made him angry all over again. It was a miracle that he had found her in one piece. Didn't she have any sense at all?

"You're going to start lecturing me again, aren't you?"

"You have no business being out here on your own. You're totally unskilled. Why didn't you tell me the truth back at Rosehill? Why did you lie?"

"I didn't want to lie to you."

"Then why did you?"

She moved away from him and leaned back against the tree again. "My problems aren't your concern. Your brothers made you come after me, didn't they?"

The question was so ludicrous he felt like laughing. "I'm here because I want to be here. Who wants to hurt you?"

"Besides you?"

"Answer me, Genevieve."

"No one wants to hurt me."

Her hands were clenched in her lap.

"Do you ever tell the truth?" he asked.

"Yes, I usually do," she replied. "But this is my problem, not yours, and I don't want you to get involved."

"Too bad. I'm already involved."

She shook her head. He nodded. "You are going to tell me everything."

"No, I'm not, and you have no business trying to interfere in my life. You could get hurt or maybe even killed, God forbid. I can't let that happen. The less you know, the better. My problems aren't your concern."

"According to Lottie, whoever is chasing you is coming to Rosehill. That makes it my concern."

"That won't happen. I left the ranch so they wouldn't track me there. I made sure I was seen leaving Blue Belle, and I left an easy trail to follow when I headed west."

"Then you backtracked to go south."

"Yes."

"Tell me about Lottie. Who is she?"

"A friend I met when she joined the choir. She's very nice, but she tends to overreact."

"Is that so?"

"Honestly, no one wants to hurt me."

His hand dropped down on top of hers. "You are going to tell me all about the trouble you're in, but first tell me who is coming after you."

She was too tired to keep on fencing with him, and he was as relentless as a devil after a soul.

"The preacher is coming after me."

He raised an eyebrow. "The preacher?"

"His name is Ezekiel Jones. It isn't his real name though. One day he decided he had a calling, and he changed his name to Ezekiel to make himself sound more important. He and three others visited the church I regularly attended. . . . I think I mentioned to you that your Mama Rose used to go to that church too. That's where I met her," she thought to add. "I never asked her, but I'm sure she liked Ezekiel. Everyone liked him. He was very charismatic and smooth talking."

A tear slipped down her cheek. Adam let out a sigh, put his arm around her shoulders, and hauled her up against him.

"Why is the preacher chasing you?"

"I sang in his choir."

He squeezed her to get her to continue. She really was an exasperating woman. Getting information out of her was a difficult undertaking, but fortunately he was a patient man. He reminded himself of that fact when the silence continued.

She outlasted him. "He wants to hurt you because you sang in his choir."

"I really don't think he wants to hurt me," she insisted. "He just wants me back."

"Why?"

"I'm his meal ticket. When I sing in his choir, the attendance goes up."

"Ah, now I understand. The donations also go up, don't they?"

She nodded. "People seem to like my voice." She sounded embarrassed to admit such a thing.

"I can see why they would."

She smiled. "You can?"

"Yeah, I can," he said.

"Do you know what, Adam? You make me feel very safe."

He laughed. Now that he knew what her problem was, his anger diminished. The trouble wasn't serious after all. It was just a nuisance, and one he would quickly deal with.

"I make you feel safe? If you knew some of the

thoughts I was having about you on my way here, you wouldn't feel that way."

She couldn't tell if he was teasing her or not. "What were you thinking?"

"Never mind. Have you told me everything?"

"Yes, of course I have."

"You didn't leave anything out?"

"Lord, you're suspicious," she said. "I'm not keeping any secrets from you. You know everything there is to know. Truly," she added with a nod.

"If you were telling me the truth—"

"I was," she interrupted.

"Then it's a very simple problem to solve."

"It is?"

The eagerness in her voice made him smile. "Yes, it is," he assured her. "I can't figure out why you didn't tell me about Ezekiel when we were at Rosehill. It would have made things easier."

"I explained why I didn't confide in you. I didn't want you to get involved. Ezekiel Jones isn't a very nice man, Adam. He won't take no for an answer."

"Did you tell him no?"

She rolled her eyes heavenward. "I certainly did."

"And?"

"He locked me in a room."

"Is that so?" he asked in a voice that was soft and chilling.

The look that came into his eyes frightened her, and she realized once again what a dangerous adversary he could be. She was suddenly very happy that he was on her side.

"Yes," she said. She rubbed her arms to ward off the chill and added, "I had to climb out a window to get away from him and his two henchmen. I tore my best skirt."

"I really wish you had said something sooner. If you didn't want to confide in me, you could have told Harrison about Ezekiel. He's an attorney, and I'm sure he could have taken some sort of legal action to discourage the man."

"Could he keep Ezekiel from following me or threatening me?"

"No, but I could," he told her quietly.

"How?"

He wouldn't explain. She worried about his intentions for several minutes and then shook her head. "I don't want you to do anything. Ezekiel can't possibly know where I am now, and when I get to Salt Lake and board the train to New York, I'll be rid of him once and for all."

"Genevieve, if I found you, why do you think the preacher won't?"

"Because you've lived in the mountains most of your life and you know how to track, but Ezekiel has always lived in the city. He won't find me, and he certainly won't follow me to the East Coast just to get me back in his choir."

"Salt Lake isn't right around the corner. You're going to have to go into Gramby, then over to Juniper Falls, turn south again and pass through Middleton, swing east through Crawford, and then it's a straight shot down into Salt Lake. Unless you plan to ride hard, that's a good four days away from here. Jones could catch up to you in any one of those towns."

"If he were following me."

"Would you worry if you knew he was only a day behind you?"

"Yes, I would. He can be a real nuisance. If he were tracking me, would you know it?"

Of course he'd know. After living in the territory for so many years, a man developed a sixth sense about such things. The skin on the back of his neck would begin to prickle, and an uneasiness would settle in his bones until he backtracked to make certain his instincts were right. Adam had done just that while he'd been following Genevieve, and that was how he had known that Ezekiel and two others were following her all right. Jones might not know how to track someone down, but one of his cohorts certainly knew what he was doing. If Genevieve stayed right where she was, the three of them would catch up with her by late tomorrow afternoon.

Adam considered telling her about Jones now, then decided to let her get a good night's sleep first. She looked exhausted and needed rest. She could worry all she wanted tomorrow.

She waited for him to answer her question, but he changed the subject instead.

"You could take the coach from Gramby, and it will take you all the way to Salt Lake. Do you have enough money to buy a ticket? You mentioned you were low on funds," he reminded her.

"I have just enough to buy the train ticket."

"You should ride in the coach. I'll give you what I have with me, but it isn't much. The bank was closed when I left Blue Belle, and I didn't want to wait."

She yawned again, apologized, and then told him in no uncertain terms that she wouldn't take a cent from him. "I've never borrowed anything from anyone, and I'm not going to start now. I'll make do."

Her head dropped down on his shoulder. He was trying to concentrate on the conversation, but she'd cuddled up against him, and her soft, warm body was proving to be one giant distraction. She smelled so good to him, and her skin was just as silky and smooth as he'd guessed it would be. He trailed his fingers down her arm and smiled when he felt her shiver.

She was as warm as a kitten and as stubborn as a mule.

"I'm very happy you came after me, and I'll be sorry to see you leave when we get to Gramby. You will have to escort me that far," she added with a nod.

"Is that right?"

"You'll worry about me if you don't go with me to Gramby. Think of it as an adventure, Adam."

"You like adventures, don't you?"

"Yes, I do."

"Then you should be happy you aren't getting married. You'd have to settle down."

"With the right man, marriage would be the most wonderful adventure of all, and when I find him, I'm never going to let go."

He was sorry he'd brought up the topic of marriage. The thought of any other man having such an adventure with Genevieve irritated him. He felt possessive toward her and couldn't understand why.

"Get some sleep, Genevieve. You're tired."

She closed her eyes. "I haven't slept much in the past couple of days."

"You aren't going to sleep sitting up, are you? Don't you have a bedroll with you?"

"Yes, but I don't want to use it."

"Don't be ridiculous. I'll get it for you."

"No," she told him in a near shout. She put her hand on his thigh to stop him from getting up.

She'd sounded as though she was in a panic. Puzzled by her bizarre reaction, he asked, "Why not?"

"Snakes," she suddenly blurted out.

"What about them?"

"They slither under the cover and curl up against your feet."

"Has that ever happened to you?"

"No, but it could, and I'm not willing to take the chance. I'm very comfortable where I am, and I would appreciate it if you didn't touch my bedroll. I spent over an hour rolling up my dresses just so inside, and they'll get wrinkled if you unroll it."

He gave up trying to reason with her. If she wanted to sit up all night, that was fine with him.

"You're a very stubborn woman."

"No, I'm not. I'm sensible."

He snorted in disbelief. She decided to ignore him and tried to go to sleep.

Adam took care of his horse, then got his own bedroll and put it on the ground on the opposite side of the fire. After adding more wood to the flames, he stretched out on top of his cover, stacked his hands behind his head, and stared up at the black sky while he thought about how he would handle the Reverend Ezekiel Jones and his friends.

"Adam?"

"I thought you were asleep."

"Almost," she whispered. "May I ask you something?"

"Sure. What do you want to know?"

"Did you ever think of marrying me?"

"No, I didn't."

His answer was quick and brutally honest, but she didn't seem to be offended by his admission.

He watched her for a long time. He couldn't figure out why he was so drawn to her, and if he hadn't known better, he would have thought he was acting like a man who was falling in love.

The possibility made him uneasy. He was content with his life, he reminded himself, and he wasn't going to change a thing.

He was just drifting off to sleep when she spoke to him again.

"I dreamed about you."

Six

He figured he would have to take her as far as Gramby. It was the least he could do, and there really wasn't any other choice. She was right: he would worry about her if he didn't go along. Besides, he'd never hear the end of it from his family—and he had a sneaking suspicion they'd find out—if he didn't accompany her and make certain she got on the coach. He had considered dragging her back to Rosehill and letting Harrison take some sort of legal action against Jones and his friends to discourage them from harassing her, but he was pretty sure Genevieve would take off again and he'd just end up chasing her.

He felt responsible for her because she was all alone. Like it or not, he was temporarily bound to her, and though it was completely out of character for him to do so, he was determined to interfere in her life.

She'd dreamed about him. He couldn't seem to get past that startling announcement. If she had meant to stun him with it, she'd succeeded magnificently.

Speechless, he'd simply stared at her and waited for her to explain why she would have done such a thing. She fell asleep instead.

She didn't wake up when he lifted her into his arms and carried her to his bedroll. He got her settled and sat down next to her. After removing his boots, he stretched his legs out, rested his shoulders against a tree, and closed his eyes.

Even in sleep she tormented him. She rolled over and curled up against his side, and just as he was dozing off, her hand dropped down in his lap. He was suddenly wide awake again. He quickly removed her hand, but less than a minute later, it was back, only this time it landed much closer to his groin. He gritted his teeth in frustration and tried to block the impossible thoughts that came into his mind. He could have gotten up and moved to the other side of the camp, but for some reason he felt compelled to stay close to her.

Needless to say, he didn't get much sleep that night.

He was up before dawn; she didn't wake up for two more hours. She was cheerful and refreshed; he was out of sorts and surly. She liked to talk in the morning; he preferred silence.

By noon, Adam had come to the conclusion that they were as different as night and day. When he wanted to get somewhere, he didn't let anything distract him. She wanted to stop and smell every flower along the way.

He rarely smiled; she laughed a lot. Mostly she laughed at him for being so overly protective toward her. She didn't seem to worry about anything and told him she thought he worried far too much.

The biggest difference between them was their attitude toward strangers. He was instinctively wary and distrustful. She was the complete opposite. Her trust in her fellow man astonished him. She greeted everyone she met as though he were a long lost friend, and she spent entirely too much time in conversation.

When they stopped to rest the horses, he reminded her of what she had told him back at Rosehill.

"'You can't trust anyone these days,'" he said. "Remember telling me that?"

"I do remember, but I meant to say that I can't trust anyone in a position of power these days. How long before we reach Gramby?"

"That all depends on you. If you insist on stopping to talk to every stranger we pass on the road, we won't get there until tomorrow."

"And if I don't talk to anyone?"

"Gramby's about five hours away. If we ride hard, we could be there before supper."

She nudged her horse forward so she could ride beside him. "Do I have a choice? If so, I think I'd prefer to take my time. I like meeting new people and hearing their stories. I think you do too."

He smiled in spite of himself. "I do?"

"Yes," she insisted. "I looked through the books in your library, and I remember seeing quite a few biographies. You obviously enjoy reading about other people's experiences. I like to read about them too, but I also like to hear firsthand about their adventures, and if you show an interest, complete strangers will tell you the most wonderful stories. Of course, you'll have to put them at ease first, which means you're going to have to stop frowning all the time and looking so threatening. People tend to shy away from armed men who look like they're going to shoot them if they say the wrong thing. Do you have any idea how intimidating you are? You're such a big man, and surely you've noticed how strangers back away from you. Maybe if you put your guns away—"

He wouldn't let her finish. "No," he told her in a voice that didn't leave room for negotiation.

She shook her head. "There isn't any polite way to tell you this. You scare people." He laughed. She didn't know what to make of that. "Do you want to scare people?"

"I haven't given it any thought, but, yes, I suppose I do."

"Why?"

"They'll give me a wide berth, that's why. I've learned not to trust anyone, and until I put you on the coach in Gramby, I'm responsible for keeping you safe."

"No, you aren't responsible for me."

He wasn't going to argue with her. "So you would rather sleep outside again tonight?"

"I don't see any reason to rush."

"What about Ezekiel Jones? Aren't you worried about him?"

"No," she answered. "He's given up looking for me by now."

It was the perfect opportunity to tell her that she was wrong and that Ezekiel was indeed following her, but once again Adam was silent. He didn't want her to fret, and if she knew he intended to talk to Ezekiel, she would probably pitch a fit. The preacher scared her, and Adam was determined to put a stop to his harassment as soon as possible.

She had been saying something to him, but he hadn't been paying any attention. The expectant look she gave him now indicated she was waiting for an answer. He had to ask her to repeat the question.

"I said I don't have a schedule to maintain, but you do, don't you? I'll bet you have a hundred things to do when you get back home."

"There's always work to be done."

"Your brothers will run the ranch while you're away. They're probably very pleased that you finally left Rosehill. I know for a fact that you've never gone anywhere outside of the mountains surrounding your ranch."

"And how would you know that?"

"I read all your letters to Mama Rose, remember? You got so busy building the ranch you forgot about your dream. By the way, Adam, I haven't made up my mind if I want to take the coach to Salt Lake or not. It seems like a waste of good money. I have a sound horse," she added. She leaned forward in her saddle to give the mare a pat of affection.

"I was a boy when I wrote those letters, and you are taking the coach."

"You wrote most of the letters when you were a boy, but there were also some that you wrote just a couple of years ago."

His response was a shrug of indifference. They rode along in silence, each caught up in thought. About fifteen miles outside of town they passed a family traveling on foot, following a wagon laden with their possessions. Genevieve stayed by Adam's side until they had reached the crest of the hill, then abruptly turned her mare around and headed back. He didn't have any choice but to follow her.

He caught up with her just in time to hear her invite the strangers to dine with her. There were five in all, a young couple with two little girls about the age of five or six, and an elderly man Adam assumed was the grandfather and patriarch of the family. The little girls stared up in fascination at Genevieve, but their mother stared at the grandfather while she awaited his decision. There was a look of eagerness and desperation on her face.

The two men were warily studying Adam. The younger one gathered his daughters up and pushed them behind his back. The protective gesture wasn't lost on Adam. If he had had children of his own and a stranger had ridden up to him with a rifle across his lap, he probably would have done the same thing. It was always better to be safe than sorry.

The little girls weren't frightened of him though. They didn't give him the time of day. They were giggling as they peeked out to look up at Genevieve.

"Adam, I would like you to meet Mr. James Meadows and his family."

The elderly man stepped forward. He was tall, painfully thin, and had snow white hair. Adam judged him to be around sixty-five or seventy years old.

As soon as Genevieve introduced the old man, he moved forward and reached up to offer his hand to Adam.

Adam shook it. "It's a pleasure to meet you, sir."

"Folks back home call me James, and I'd be pleasured if you'd do the same," he said in a voice that was thick with a southern twang. "This here is my son, Will, and his wife, Ellie. Those two little chatterboxes are Annie and Jessie. You can see they're twins," he added proudly. "Jessie's the one missing her front teeth."

Will stepped forward to shake Adam's hand. He was a strapping man with broad shoulders and brawny hands. After sizing him up, Adam decided that Will was used to doing hard labor out in the sun, for he had bulging muscles in his forearms and weather-beaten skin.

"Are you a gunslinger?" Will asked, frowning over the possibility.

Adam shook his head. "No, I'm a rancher."

Will didn't look as though he believed him. Genevieve gave Adam an I-told-you-so look before turning back to the Meadows family.

"Adam does look like a gunslinger, but he really is a rancher. He and his brothers own quite a large spread outside of Blue Belle."

"You own the land?" James asked Adam.

"Yes, sir, I do," Adam replied.

James gave his son a quick nod of encouragement. The younger man immediately stepped forward again. He tried not to sound overly eager when he asked, "Would you be looking to hire some extra hands?"

"I can always use more help," Adam said. "Are you looking for a job?"

"Yes, sir, I am," Will answered. "I can put in a long day doing any job you give me, and I won't stop until I get it done. I'm a good worker, sir, and I'm strong, real strong."

"Ranching is hard work," Adam warned.

"I'm not afraid of it," Will replied.

"Then you've got a job," Adam told him.

"We're headed for a new beginning. Jobs have dried up down south," he explained. "Where exactly might this ranch of yours be?"

Adam gave them directions to Rosehill. "It will take you a good two weeks to walk all that way. I should be back home by then, but in the event I'm not, just tell my brother Cole you're there to work."

"We'll make it without any trouble at all," Will promised.

His wife grabbed hold of his arm and hugged him. There were tears in her eyes, and she was frantically trying to blink them away.

"I might be useful for you to hire too," James said. "I've got a few good years of work left in me."

"Why don't we talk about this during lunch?" Genevieve suggested.

James looked as if he was about to decline the invitation. Adam thought he knew why. The family had obviously hit hard times, and they had probably used up all of their money too. They were dressed in clothes that were so worn they should have been thrown out. The little girls were barefoot, but aside from the dirt on the bottoms of their feet, they were spotlessly clean.

All of them looked in dire need of a good meal.

Genevieve wasn't going to take no for an answer. "We were planning to have a picnic," she announced. "And we would love for you to join us. There's plenty of food, and I don't want it to go to waste. Isn't that right, Adam?"

The entire family turned to hear his reply.

"Yes, that's right," he said.

"We'd be pleased to join you," James announced with a nod.

Will and Ellie shared a smile. Genevieve beamed with pleasure. Adam knew she was relieved. She had obviously been worried about the family. She had seen the condition of their clothing and had assumed, as he had, that they were hungry, but unlike him, she had rushed forward to do something about it. Her generosity and compassion humbled him, and he no longer minded the delay in their journey at all.

They ate lunch by a stream about a half a mile south of the main road. While Adam took care of their horses, Ellie helped Genevieve spread the blanket on the ground and put the food out. There was cheese, salted ham, biscuits, apples, dried bananas, and sugar cookies for dessert. They drank cold water from the stream. Although Genevieve had enough food for all of them, she didn't eat much at all. She seemed content to nibble on a biscuit, and as soon as everyone had eaten their fill, she insisted they take most of the leftover food with them, using the excuse that she would have to throw it away if they didn't.

"How does a man like yourself end up owning a ranch?" James asked.

Adam shrugged. He wasn't used to telling anyone about his personal life. Private to the extreme, he decided to tell them that owning the ranch was a result of hard work and a lot of luck. Genevieve had other ideas. She decided to tell his life story.

He was too astonished to interrupt. She knew

everything about him, which really wasn't all that surprising, since she had read his letters and Mama Rose would have filled in the gaps. What stunned him was the fact that she remembered so many details that even he had forgotten. She had a way with words, and by the time she was finished, she had romanticized the story until he barely recognized himself. She made him out to be a champion, a warrior, and a hero, and from the look in her eyes as she gazed at him and the sound of her voice as she spoke, he couldn't help but think that she really believed he was all those things.

The Meadowses were captivated by the tale. They stared up at him as though he had just grown a halo over his head. He gave Genevieve a look to let her know she was going to catch hell when they were alone. She smiled back at him.

Adam thought he and Genevieve should head for Gramby. Genevieve thought they should stay and visit for a spell. Will and James were full of questions about Rosehill. While Adam answered them, Genevieve sat by his side. She waited for a lull in the conversation and then suggested that he give Will and James an advance against their wages to secure their positions.

Adam knew what her real motive was. They needed money to replenish their supplies. Realizing how important it was for a man to hold on to his pride, she had come up with a solution that would be acceptable to them. James and Will both protested, and Genevieve must have thought that Adam was going to let them have their way, because she put her hand on his arm and pinched him.

He kept his attention centered on the grandfather while he put his hand down on top of hers and squeezed hard. She let out a little yelp and pulled away.

"If you work for me, you take the advance," he told both men.

"Is that how it's done at Rosehill?" Will asked.

"Yes," Genevieve blurted out.

Adam handed each man twenty dollars. "I expect to see you at the ranch by the end of the month."

He shook their hands to seal the bargain, told Genevieve it was time to leave, and then started to get up.

James Meadows changed his mind with his next remark. "Adam, you've got the same noble look in your eyes that President Abraham Lincoln had when I saw him. Yes, sir, you do."

Astounded, he asked, "You saw Lincoln?"

"I sure did."

Adam wanted to hear every detail. He sat back down, and for the next hour he listened in rapt fascination as James shared his remarkable experience of seeing the man Adam personally believed was the greatest orator and president of all time.

"He was on his way to Gettysburg," James said. "It was a terrible time back then. The war had already taken so many young men. Folks were scared, and rightly so, and when the war finally ended, everyone flooded into the cities looking for work. It was bad for a long spell, but then it got better for a while."

"And now it's bad again," Will interjected.

"Where is home?" Adam asked.

"The prettiest little spot in the whole country," James boasted. "Norfolk, Virginia."

"Rosehill is very pretty too," Genevieve said. "I'm sure you're going to like living there, and soon you'll think of the town of Blue Belle as home."

"I'm sure we will," James agreed with a smile before turning back to Adam and asking him if he had ever been to Gettysburg.

"No, I haven't," Adam replied.

"I walked the fields of battle," James announced.

Adam wanted to hear all about it. He was impressed that James remembered the battles and the dates. He also knew details Adam had never read about.

While the men discussed the war, the twins took turns sitting on Genevieve's lap. She braided their hair and used the pink ribbons from the sleeves of her dress to tie bows for each of them. Ellie sat by her side. She and Genevieve whispered back and forth, and every now and then Genevieve would nod.

Adam kept glancing over at her. He heard one of the twins tell her she was pretty. He silently agreed.

It was going on three in the afternoon when Adam finally pulled Genevieve to her feet and insisted they get going.

James followed them to their horses. "If you don't mind my asking, how long have you two been married? You're newlyweds, aren't you?"

Genevieve laughed. Adam frowned.

"What makes you think we're newlyweds?" she asked.

"The way he looks at you," James replied.

"How exactly do I look at her?" Adam wanted to know.

"Like you haven't quite figured her out. You're puzzled, but you like what you're seeing, and that's about the same way I used to look at my bride, God rest her soul. Come to think about it, I guess I looked at her that very same way until the day she died. I never did figure that woman out, so I guess you could say we were newlyweds for close to thirty-two years."

Genevieve thought that was the sweetest thing she had ever heard. "What a lovely tribute to your late wife," she whispered, fairly overcome with emotion.

"I didn't mean to make you weepy about it," he replied. "If the two of you are considering sleeping outside, you might want to camp over by Blue Glass Lake. It's mighty pretty over there, and peaceful. You two will have all the privacy you could want."

Genevieve waited for Adam to tell James that they

weren't married. He didn't say a word, and when she nudged him and looked up at him, he ignored her.

"We're going to stay in Gramby," he said.

"Why is it called Blue Glass Lake?" she asked.

"Because the water looks like blue glass," James answered. "It's deep, but you can see all the way to the rock bottom, and you can sit on the bank and actually see the fish swimming around. Someone tied a rope to one of the branches that hangs out over the water. I expect so you can swing out and drop down in the center of the lake, but my granddaughters are too young and too timid to try, and Will and Ellie weren't inclined."

Genevieve turned to Adam. He was already shaking his head.

"Wouldn't we—"

"No," he interrupted. "We're going to Gramby."

Seven

&

Blue Glass Lake was breathtakingly beautiful. James Meadows certainly hadn't exaggerated, but Genevieve was surprised he hadn't mentioned the trees, for they were even more glorious. Like towering sentinels keeping watch, they surrounded the lake on all sides. They were so thick in some spots it wasn't possible to squeeze through the openings between the trunks. Long branches arched gracefully across the expanse of water, and like the fingers of a lady's hands, they were elegantly entwined. The sun dappled on the leaves, and in the soft breeze they glittered like diamonds.

Adam told her the oaks were at least a hundred years old. He sat down on the ground with his rifle across his lap and leaned back against a fat tree trunk, smiling as he watched her try to get a foothold so she could climb up to fetch the rope hanging from one of the lower branches.

Her skirts hindered her movements, and after trying several times, she gave up.

"Now, aren't you happy we decided to make the detour?" she asked.

"I'm happy you quit hounding me," he teased.

"Look what you would have missed," she told him. She put her hands up and twirled around in a circle. "It's a paradise."

He silently agreed. He felt as though he had just entered a magical land. Spring's vibrant colors surrounded him, and he knew that if he had seen a painting of this idyllic spot, he wouldn't have believed that it really existed. Yet here it was in all of its perfection, and for a short while the beauty belonged to him.

He stared at Genevieve and decided that she belonged in such a place. Her surroundings enhanced her beauty. The joy in her face, so innocent and pure, made his breath catch in the back of his throat.

"What are you thinking about?" she asked.

She sat down beside him and began to untie her shoelaces, but then glanced up at him when he hesitated in answering.

"I was thinking that you never take anything for granted."

"I've learned not to," she replied quietly.

"How did you learn not to?" he asked.

Her shoulders sagged. She removed one shoe and started on the other. "Family," she whispered. "So many people go through their lives with blinders on. They become self-involved and only want to think about their wants and their desires. They don't leave room for anything else, and then, too late, they realize how important their families were."

"Were you like that?" he asked.

"Yes, I was," she replied. "I was so busy getting where I thought I wanted to go I didn't make time for the people who loved me. Now they're gone."

The sadness he heard in her voice made him want

to put his arms around her and comfort her. When she leaned against him, he gave in to the urge and pulled her close.

"I'm sure your family was very proud of you."

"Yes, they were proud of me, but I'm not sure they really knew what to make of me. I rarely came home for a visit, and when I did, I never stayed more than a night or two. I would be all decked out in the latest fashions, and I tried to act so sophisticated. I called them 'mother dear' and 'father dear,' and now that I look back, I realize they exhibited an amazing amount of patience with me. I'm not sure if I was trying to impress them or myself. I never took time to think about it. I was so busy back then chasing fame and fortune." She shook her head and then added, "What a waste of precious time."

"Genevieve, I'm sure they understood."

"Perhaps," she agreed. "I didn't understand them though. My father put in a lovely garden in the front of the house, and every evening after supper he and my mother would tend it. They spent hours there. It was lovely," she added. "They had every flower you could imagine blooming, and on the fence were roses. Red roses. I used to think my parents led such boring lives, and now . . . ."

"Now what?" he asked.

"I want to have a garden of my own someday just like theirs. I don't want to waste time. I want to appreciate every minute, and I want to teach my children to do the same thing."

"I thought you longed for adventure."

"Living is an adventure, Adam. Look around you. Being here is an adventure, and we would have missed it if we had hurried to Gramby."

He laughed. "Point taken."

"I love the fact that it's so secluded. Right this minute, this beautiful spot belongs to us and no one else."

He also liked the seclusion, though for a different reason. Blue Glass Lake was so far off the beaten path Ezekiel Jones and his friends wouldn't find them here. On their way to the lake, Adam had led her through a creek bed so that their tracks couldn't be followed, and he was certain no one was going to intrude on them now.

She shrugged his arm off of her. "I'm going swimming if the water isn't too cold. Would you like to join me?"

"Maybe later," he replied.

She turned away from him to remove her socks, then stood up and ran to the water's edge.

"It looks deep," she called out. She lifted the hem of her skirt and tested the water with her toes. It was surprisingly warm and too inviting to resist. Had she been alone, she would have taken her skirt and blouse off and swum in her underclothes. Since Adam was watching her like a hawk, she was going to have to keep everything on.

She turned around to face him, put her arms out wide, closed her eyes, and then fell backward.

She could hear him laughing when she came up for air. The sound echoed through the trees around her. She would have laughed with him, but she was too busy trying to stay afloat. Her skirt and petticoats had absorbed quite a bit of water and were weighing her down. She was able to swim, but she stayed close to the bank, and after fifteen minutes or so, she was exhausted.

Getting into the water had been much easier than getting out. She made three attempts before she gave up.

All she had to do was call to him and he was there. He reached down with one hand and pulled her out of the lake with incredible ease.

He didn't let go of her. Honest to God, he tried, but his hands seemed to have a will of their own. They slid around her waist and pulled her up tight against his chest.

Her clothes were plastered to her, and she was dripping wet. He didn't mind. Her head was tilted back, and all he wanted to think about was kissing every inch of her perfect neck. No, that wasn't true. He wanted to do a whole lot more than simply kiss her.

Her hands were pressed against his chest. She could feel his heart beating under her fingertips, and she had the almost overwhelming desire to caress him. She blamed the urge on him. The way he was looking at her made her shiver with excitement. He was so serious and intense.

She stared into his eyes and felt as though she were drowning under his dark, sensual scrutiny. Was he going to kiss her? He was frowning, and she didn't think he wanted to, but, oh, God, she would die if he didn't.

"Adam?" she whispered. "What's come over you?"

He shook his head. How could he tell her that he thought she had cast a spell on him and he didn't know how much longer he was going to be able to resist her? From the moment he'd met her, she had ruled his every thought.

The infatuation had to end. "You'll be leaving tomorrow," he said, his voice rough, angry.

"Yes, I will," she whispered.

"We'll never see each other again."

"No, we won't," she agreed.

She was making circles on his chest with her fingertips. The feathery light caress was driving him crazy.

"It's for the best." He was slowly pulling her arms up around his neck.

"Yes, it's for the best," she said.

His frown deepened. "My life's all mapped out, Genevieve. I don't have time for you."

"I don't have time for you either," she told him. *Liar, liar,* she silently chanted. "Adam? Are you going to kiss me?"

"Hell, no."

And then his mouth came down on top of hers, and it was the most amazing kiss she had ever experienced. His mouth was warm and firm and wonderful. He nibbled at her lips until she opened her mouth, and then his tongue slipped inside, and, oh, Lord, that was even more glorious. She clutched handfuls of his shirt and held on for dear life while he slowly, meticulously devoured her.

The kiss seemed endless, and he didn't lift his head away from hers until he had taken every ounce of her strength. She sagged against him and closed her eyes.

Her head rested in the crook of his neck. She sighed into his ear. "Are you going to want to kiss me again?" she asked dreamily.

"No."

"It was very nice," she whispered.

She kissed the side of his neck and felt him shudder. Then he slowly pulled her arms away from him. The moment was over.

"Tomorrow you're going to get on that coach and I'm going to go back home."

"I know," she replied. "I'm going to Kansas."

"No, you're not. You're going to Paris."

"Yes, Paris."

He put his hands on her shoulders and took a step back. She had a bemused look on her face, and damn if he didn't want to kiss her again.

He made himself turn away from her instead. "I shouldn't have kissed you. It won't happen again."

"I wouldn't mind . . ."

"I'd mind," he snapped. He softened his voice when he next spoke. "You're shivering. You should get out of those wet clothes."

"That isn't why I'm shivering."

"I'll build a fire."

Those were the last words he said to her for a very long time. She thought he was probably thinking about all the work he had to do when he returned to Rosehill.

The long day had worn her out. Wrapped in a blanket he had given her, she fell asleep and didn't wake up until the following morning.

After a breakfast of fresh fish, Adam saddled the horses while she put the supplies away. They left paradise a few minutes later. Thunder rumbled in the distance, and the sky became an omen of what was to come.

Eight

$\mathcal{T}$rouble was brewing in Gramby.

The pretty little town was nestled high up in the shoulder of the mountains. Several years ago the population had swelled considerably when rumors circulated that there was gold to be found in the surrounding hills and creek beds. The Pickerman Hotel had been constructed during that booming period, as had countless other buildings, but as luck would have it, the rumors turned out to be false, and as quickly as folks had hightailed it into town, they packed up their belongings and hightailed it out. Now there were more buildings than people to occupy them.

Hard times called for hard measures. The Pickerman Hotel was rarely full, but every once in a while, when he became desperate enough, Ernest Pickerman would join forces with his arch enemy, Harry Steeple, the owner of the neighboring saloon. The two men would pool their money and pay outrageous sums to entice entertainers to come to their town. What made their collaboration remarkable was the fact that Pickerman and Steeple had been trying to kill each other for years. Neither could abide the sight of the other, but business was business, they both agreed, and they could put off feuding until their coffers were refilled.

They had a gentleman's agreement, but since they didn't happen to be gentlemen, the rules governing conduct didn't apply.

Pickerman and Steeple were both skating on thin ice with the rest of the folks of Gramby. Twice in the past month alone the two men had collected money from them to send for entertainers, and both times the entertainers hadn't bothered to show up. It never occurred to either man to give refunds, which made them extremely unpopular fellows with the good citizens, but Pickerman and Steeple were about to redeem themselves by pulling off their greatest coup of all time.

Adam and Genevieve just happened to ride into town on the day that Miss Ruby Leigh Diamond—showgirl extraordinaire, as she was billed—was expected to perform at the Gold and Glitter Saloon. The folks of Gramby were suspicious that they were once again about to be fleeced, but they still paid in advance for tickets on the off chance that Ruby Leigh would show up. Word had spread like smallpox, and folks had flooded into the town from as far as fifty miles away. They were also willing to pay an exorbitant price to get a peek, or gander, depending on where they were seated, at Ruby Leigh's spectacular legs.

The two mismatched entrepreneurs had worked out all the arrangements so that there wouldn't be any problems. Pickerman would personally take Ruby Leigh from the coach to her hotel room. When she was rested and ready, he would escort her halfway down the boardwalk, where Steeple would be waiting, then step back and hand her over to him. Neither man had set foot in the other's establishment in over ten years, and not even a pair of magnificent legs would make them break that important tradition.

Gramby was the turning point for the stagecoach. It came up from Salt Lake City once a week, then turned around and went back. On Tuesday morning, the coach arrived right on schedule, at ten o'clock in the morning. Pickerman was ready. With a flourish and a prayer, he stepped off the boardwalk and prepared to open the door. Sweat dotted his brow and his palms, and saliva filled his mouth in anticipation of being the first man in Gramby to gaze upon Ruby Leigh Diamond's curvaceous legs when she alighted from the coach.

Unfortunately, Ruby Leigh's legs were missing, and so was the rest of her. For a minute, Pickerman refused to accept that she wasn't inside. He stuck his head in to make certain she hadn't gotten stuck in a crevice somewhere. Then he started cursing and spitting. Panic quickly set in as soon as he spotted a number of people hurrying toward the coach. He slammed the door shut, shouted to the driver to move along, and then ran inside the hotel.

An immediate conference was called. The two owners met in the alley between their establishments to decide what to do. They knew they would be strung up from the nearest tree if they didn't produce the goods, and so they furiously tried to come up with an acceptable story.

The pity was that even though they put their heads together, they still didn't have enough brains between them to think of anything remotely plausible.

And so they lied. Everyone who stopped by the hotel or the saloon that day was told that Ruby Leigh Diamond had already arrived.

By six o'clock that evening, Pickerman had gone through three handkerchiefs mopping the sweat from his brow. Steeple had worn two blisters on his toes from pacing around his saloon in his brand-new two-toned shoes. He decided that the only way he was going to be able to keep that noose from slipping around his neck was to blame Pickerman and shoot him down like a mad dog before the truth came out. Ironically, Pickerman had come up with the very same idea.

They took off with their guns blazing and had each other pinned down outside of town in Tommy Murphy's tomato field. They were so busy trying to kill each other they almost let a golden opportunity ride past. Pickerman just happened to jump up from behind the rock where he had been hiding, with the intention of putting a bullet in Steeple's backside because it was the biggest and easiest target he could find, when out of the corner of his eye he saw a beautiful woman on horseback trotting by.

He called an immediate truce by waving his soggy handkerchief in the air with one hand and pointing his pistol toward the beautiful woman in the distance with his other hand.

Steeple caught on to Pickerman's plan right away. "We've been saved," he shouted.

"She could be our manna from heaven," Pickerman shouted back.

In unison, the men tucked their guns in their pants and ran to intercept her before she got away. They were running so fast the heels of their shoes smacked their backsides. When they came barreling around the corner of the dirt road that led into town, they spotted Adam and immediately stopped dead in their tracks.

Steeple put his hands up in the air to let the big stranger know he didn't mean to do any harm. Pickerman mopped his brow but kept a wary eye on the woman's companion.

"Wait up, miss," Steeple shouted. "We got a proposition for you."

"It's a moneymaker," Pickerman bellowed.

Genevieve reined her horse in. Adam shook his head at her and told her to keep going.

"Aren't you the least bit curious?" she asked while she waited for the two strangers to catch up with her.

"No," he answered.

"He mentioned money," she said. "You have to be low on funds, and I'm completely out. It would be foolish of me not to listen to what they have to say," she added.

Adam was incredulous. "You don't have any money at all?"

"No, I—"

"You gave it away, didn't you?"

"Now, why would you—"

"Did you?" he demanded.

"As a matter of fact, I did. I had to," she cried out. "If you had only seen—"

She was going to tell him about the couple she had encountered on the road the day before yesterday and how desperate their situation was, but Adam didn't give her an opportunity.

"Had to give it away? Were you robbed?"

"No, I wasn't—"

"I cannot believe you would go traipsing—"

"Their need was greater than mine," she interrupted. "And I don't traipse anywhere."

He took a deep, calming breath. "Exactly how were you planning to get to Salt Lake?"

She turned back to him. "I will either ride my horse there or I will sell her and use the money to buy a ticket on the coach. I did think things through," she added.

"And if you can't get enough money to buy a ticket?"

"Then I won't sell the mare."

"What about food and shelter and—"

"Adam, it's ridiculous for you to get angry. I can always find work," she assured him.

Pickerman's huffing and puffing turned her attention. He was the first to reach her side. Steeple was hot on his heels. Adam instinctively moved his rifle across his lap. The barrel was pointed at the men.

He then ordered the strangers to step away from her.

They barely gave him a glance, for both were staring up at Genevieve with expressions of rapture on their faces.

Pickerman made the introductions. "How would you like to earn twenty whole dollars?"

Steeple poked him hard in his ribs and smiled when he heard him grunt in pain.

"You might have gotten her for ten," he muttered.

Genevieve glanced at Adam to see how he was reacting to the pair. His expression showed only mild disdain. The two men were peculiar, she thought, and complete opposites in appearance. One was tall and thin and seemed to have a problem with perspiration. His face was dripping wet. The other man was short and squat. He seemed to have a problem walking, for she noticed he was grimacing and kept hopping from foot to foot.

"What exactly did you have in mind, gentlemen?" she asked.

Steeple answered her. "We just want you to spend the evening entertaining some folks."

Adam exploded. "That's it," he roared. "Genevieve, we're leaving. As for you two—"

Pickerman raised his hands. "It ain't what it sounded like. We're in a bind, a real bind, and if the lady won't help us out, we'll be hanged for sure."

Steeple vigorously nodded. "I own the saloon next to his hotel," he said with a nod toward Pickerman. "I got a real fancy stage, and sometimes we get big-name entertainers to come here. Both of us happened to observe what a nice pair of ankles you have, miss, and we're hoping and praying your legs are just as shapely."

"You aren't going to be seeing her legs," Adam snapped.

"Steeple, shut your trap 'cause you're only making the gentleman mad every time you speak. Let me tell it," Pickerman demanded. He paused to mop his face with his handkerchief and then said, "We're in a real bad way, miss. We've already disappointed folks twice in the past month because the entertainers we sent for didn't show up. Now it's happened again. We collected money and sent for Miss Ruby Leigh Diamond to come and sing and dance at the saloon. We whet everyone's appetite by putting up signs all over town, and wouldn't you know it? She didn't come. In about an hour and a half, folks are going to start getting suspicious. They'll catch on quick when she doesn't come twirling out on stage."

"I expect they will," she agreed.

"All you got to do is pretend to be Ruby," Steeple pleaded.

"Ruby Leigh Diamond? That can't be the woman's real name," she said, trying hard not to laugh.

"Alice," Pickerman blurted out. "Her name's Alice O'Reilly."

"Then she's Irish."

"Yes, miss, she is," Steeple said.

Genevieve smiled. "I'm not Irish," she said quietly. "My ancestors came here from Africa. Surely you noticed. You cannot think anyone would think I'm Ruby Leigh Diamond, for heaven's sake. Have you lost your wits?"

"Begging your pardon, miss, but I don't think you grasp the seriousness of our predicament. We'll lose our necks if we don't find a pretty lady to go out on stage," Steeple whined. "You don't have to be Ruby if you don't want to. We can give you another stage name. How about Opal or Emerald?"

"My name is Genevieve. What exactly am I expected to do on stage?"

"Don't you see? We don't rightly care what you do. You're real pretty, and maybe if you twirl around a couple of times and sashay back and forth, folks will think they got their money's worth."

"Are you about ready to get going?" Adam asked.

She shook her head. "These gentlemen do seem to be in a bind. If I help them out, I could be saving their hides."

"Yes, miss, that's exactly right," Pickerman agreed.

She did feel sorry for them, but she was also intrigued by the possibility of replenishing her funds so quickly. It was an appealing proposition. There was a dilemma however.

"I do sing, but only in church," she explained.

"She sings, Pickerman," Steeple shouted. "It's a sign, I tell you. She was sent to us."

"There you have it," Steeple said. "You sing. That's what you'll do, then."

"Can you twirl?" Pickerman wanted to know.

Adam was shaking his head. She ignored him and asked, "Is twirling important?"

Steeple shrugged. "I expect so," he said. "Folks will want to see your ankles."

She glanced at Adam, saw his dark expression, and knew he'd reached his boiling point.

"I don't think I'll be doing any twirling or sashaying, but I would like to earn thirty dollars. I'll sing for that amount of money and not a dollar less."

The two men didn't need to discuss the matter. Steeple reached up and shook her hand. "You've got yourself a deal, little lady."

"May I have the money in advance?" she asked.

"As soon as you step out on stage, we'll give the money to your companion," Steeple told her with a nod toward Adam.

"He'll shoot you if you don't pay him," she said sweetly.

Pickerman turned to Adam. "You won't have to shoot anyone. He'll pay."

"Now all we have to do is sneak you in the back door of the saloon so folks won't know you only just got there."

"I've never been inside a saloon," she remarked.

"Well, now, this will be a treat for you," Pickerman said.

Adam's patience was all used up. "Genevieve, I'm putting my foot down. You aren't going to sing for a bunch of drunk men."

"There might be women there too," Steeple promised.

"Adam, have some compassion," Genevieve said. "These gentlemen need my help."

Both Pickerman and Steeple nodded in unison, their chins wobbling like a pair of turkeys pecking at the ground.

"People will understand if they tell them the truth," Adam said.

"We can't tell them Ruby didn't show. They'll hang us," Steeple insisted.

"Don't you have a sheriff in Gramby?" Genevieve asked.

"Yes, miss, we do," Pickerman answered. "But he isn't in Gramby today. He headed over to Middleton as soon as he heard their bank was robbed. Folks over there don't need his help though, because there are three U.S. marshals on their way to Middleton now. They'll catch the robbers quick enough."

"But Middleton's a couple of hours away, and by the time our sheriff comes back home, we'll be swingin' from the trees," Steeple said.

"You took money for tickets, didn't you?" Adam asked.

"We did," Steeple agreed.

"Then give them refunds."

The men looked horrified by the notion. "We couldn't do that," Pickerman said.

"It's bad business," Steeple interjected.

Adam gave up trying to make them be reasonable. Genevieve continued to look sympathetic.

"Miss Genevieve, do you happen to have a nice little something to wear on stage?"

She smiled. "I have just the thing."

Nine

She wore her favorite church dress. It was the color of freshly churned butter and had a matching wide-brimmed hat, wrist-length gloves, and shoes. The dress was long-sleeved and covered her ankles and her neck, and therefore met Adam's stipulations. Nevertheless, he still wasn't happy when he saw her all decked out in her Sunday finery. Neither were Steeple and Pickerman. They took turns begging her to find something else to put on.

Adam had insisted they stay at the boardinghouse outside of town, but there hadn't been time to go there to change her clothes, and so she'd ended up using Steeple's storage closet behind the stage. She made Pickerman guard the door, ignoring his protest that he was breaking a sacred vow by entering Steeple's den of iniquity. Adam and Steeple waited near the stage. When she stepped out and asked Adam if she looked all right, he shook his head and told her she would incite men's appetites wearing such a revealing garment. While Steeple pleaded with her to at least roll up her sleeves, Adam moved forward, nudged her chin up, and fastened her two top buttons.

She knew he was angry that he hadn't been able to change her mind. He knew she was nervous, because he could feel her trembling.

"It isn't too late to leave," he whispered.

She moved closer to him and tried to smile. "I am a little nervous," she admitted.

He put his arms around her, but resisted the urge to try to shake some sense into her.

"Then let's go. You don't have any business inside a saloon. You're too refined for such a place."

She thought that was a lovely thing for him to say. "I am?" she asked.

"Let's go."

She shook her head. "It's thirty whole dollars," she reminded him once again. "I could pay you back what I owe you."

"You don't owe me anything."

"I made you give your money to the Meadows family, remember?"

His head dropped down toward hers so that he could hear her whispers over the crowd's shouts coming from the other side of the stage.

"You didn't make me do anything I didn't want to do."

"For the love of God, now isn't the time to be whispering sweet nothings into each other's ears. We got a situation here," Steeple cried out.

"The audience sounds . . . restless," she said.

"It isn't an audience, it's a mob," Adam snapped.

Steeple latched onto Genevieve's arm. "If he'll unhand you, I'll show you where you should wait."

He tugged her away from Adam and then guided her over to the left side of the stage behind the red velvet drape. She had grabbed hold of Adam's hand and wouldn't let go. He kept trying to get her to change her mind, but she was in such a panic now, she could barely hear a word he said.

The noise of the crowd was deafening. Pride kept her from picking up her skirts and running for safety. She had given her word, and she meant to keep it.

She tried to look out at the audience, but Steeple saw what she was about to do and rushed forward to put himself in front of her.

The crowd was getting restless. As one, they began to chant Ruby Leigh Diamond's name and pound their fists on the tables. They hurled their empty whiskey bottles at the walls and the stage.

The noise was frightful. "They sound . . . impatient," Genevieve said when she heard a loud crash.

"Ruby . . . Ruby . . . Ruby . . ." the crowd chanted.

"You still haven't told them Ruby isn't here?" Adam demanded.

"I'm going out there now to tell them," Steeple promised. He turned to Genevieve. "After I introduce you, the band will start playing, and you come on out."

"Wait," she cried when he turned to leave. "What will they be playing?"

Steeple smiled. "Well, now, no one rightly knows. Elvin will be pounding a tune on his piano, and the two fiddlers I hired will figure it out and catch up in no time."

"But what is the song?"

"Is that important?"

"Yes," she stammered.

He patted her arm. "It'll be fine. Just fine," he promised.

Her stomach was doing flips. She thought she might be turning green too. She dared a peek out at the audience and was immediately sorry. There were two men hanging down from the balcony above, and both were pouring bottles of liquor on the cantankerous crowd below.

She jumped back and sagged against Adam's chest. "Oh, dear," she whispered.

Adam had never felt such acute frustration in his entire life. Why must Genevieve be so stubborn? Didn't she know that as soon as the crowd heard that Ruby wouldn't be performing, they would tear the place apart?

"Are you still hell-bent on this foolishness?"

Before she could answer, Pickerman came running. "You'd best get on out there," he told Steeple. "Fargus is swinging from your chandelier and cross-eyed Harry is trying to lasso him with his rope. They're both drunk as skunks."

Adam reached over Genevieve's shoulder and grabbed Steeple by his collar. "If anyone gets near her while she's out there, I'm going to shoot him. Got that?"

Steeple vigorously nodded and then scurried out on stage. She held her breath in anticipation of the crowd's reaction when they heard Ruby wasn't there.

Steeple had both his hands up with the palms out and was waving to the audience to be quiet. An expectant hush followed. Fargus let go of the chandelier and landed on top of the table to take his seat. Cross-eyed Harry dropped his rope and sat down next to his friend. He let out a loud, low belch. The crowd erupted in laughter, but quieted down again as soon as Steeple motioned to them.

"Now, men, I told you Miss Ruby Leigh Diamond would be performing tonight—"

He abruptly stopped. The crowd leaned forward and waited expectantly for him to continue. Steeple didn't say another word for a full minute. He simply stood in the center of the stage, shifting back and forth from one foot to the other, smiling at his audience as he squinted out at them. They squinted back. The seconds ticked by, and the only sound that could be heard was the squeak of Steeple's brand-new, two-toned shoes.

The audience soon grew impatient. A murmur of dissent began in the back of the saloon, and like a wave, it gathered momentum as it worked its way forward.

Just as Fargus was turning to the chandelier and his companion was reaching for his rope, a slow, sly smile came over Steeple's face.

"I promised you Ruby Leigh Diamond," he bellowed. "And here she is."

With a flourish, he bowed low to Genevieve, straightened back up, and gave Elvin the signal to start pounding on his piano. Then he ran as though lightning were chasing him to the opposite side of the stage. He ducked behind the curtain, but peeked out to see how the audience was reacting.

Pickerman slapped thirty dollars into the palm of Adam's hand, gave Genevieve a pitying glance and a quick shove toward the stage, and then ran to find a place to hide.

Adam was glaring at Steeple. "I'm going to kill that son of a—"

She interrupted him. "This *is* going to be an adventure," she whispered.

She straightened her shoulders, forced a smile, and inched her way onto the stage.

Adam went with her. He moved out just far enough to be seen by everyone. He slowly lifted his rifle, slipped his finger through the trigger ring, and pointed the barrel at the center of the crowd. His message wasn't subtle. The first man who dared to utter a single word of disappointment over the obvious fact that Genevieve wasn't Ruby was going to get shot. If the weapon wasn't a sufficient deterrent, the expression on his face was. He looked bad-tempered and trigger-happy.

As it turned out, none of his precautions were the least bit necessary.

She took their breath away. The sight of her dressed so primly in her Sunday best stunned them speechless. They stared and they gaped. Elvin stopped playing the piano; the fiddlers dropped their bows, and like everyone else in the saloon, they too stared up in openmouthed stupefaction at the woman on the stage.

She was a nervous wreck. Some adventures were better left unpursued, she thought frantically. She had to be crazy to be doing this. Adam was right. It was foolishness.

She turned to leave and saw him standing there on stage with her, with his rifle up and ready to fire and an expression on his face that would have made the fainthearted shriek.

He wasn't going to let any harm come to her. Her smile widened as she turned back to her audience. Her knees were knocking, her stomach was flipping, and her throat was closing, but all she could think about was that Adam was protecting her.

Was it any wonder why she loved this man?

Something smelled vile. It was the sinful stench of whiskey surrounding her. She looked from side to side and saw all the empty bottles littering the tables and the floor.

Her audience was drunk, shame on them, and she was suddenly too disgusted to be nervous.

The crowd was finally getting over their initial surprise. Some of the men smiled at her; others frowned. She wasn't at all what they had expected, but before any of them could get riled up about Steeple's trickery in substituting one woman for another, Genevieve began to sing.

From that moment on, she held them in the palm of her hand. Adam wouldn't have believed it if he hadn't seen it with his own eyes. Within minutes, she had turned drunken louts into simpering crybabies.

She chose to sing one of her church songs, "Come Ye Sinners, Poor and Needy." The lyrics aptly fit the audience. Her voice was so rich and vibrant it caressed the crowd and soothed the beast within them. One by one the men began to listen to the words and bow their heads. Several pushed their glasses of whiskey aside. Others took out their handkerchiefs and wiped the tears from their eyes.

By the time the song ended, everyone was weeping. Adam moved back into the shadows and lowered his rifle. He wanted to laugh, so bizarre did he find their reaction, but he didn't dare for fear the sound would break the collective mood in the saloon. He knew why she had chosen the song, of course. She wanted to shame the men, and from the way their shoulders were shaking and their heads were bobbing, it was apparent she had succeeded.

The second song was called "My Sainted Mother, Your Hopes for Me" and struck an even greater emotional chord with the crowd. By the time she was finished with the third verse, one man was bawling so loudly his friends had to hush him.

Steeple went into a panic as soon as he noticed no one was buying or drinking his high-priced liquor. He moved forward to get Genevieve's attention, and when she glanced over at him, he started seesawing his arm back and forth and snapping his fingers to let her know he wanted her to pick up the beat.

Adam did laugh then. He simply couldn't contain his amusement any longer. Genevieve smiled at Steeple and then proceeded to sing yet another song about death and redemption and sinners who finally saw the light and changed their sorry ways. Adam suspected she was making up the lyrics as she went along, because none of the words rhymed, but he seemed to be the only one who noticed.

Steeple was tearing his hair out in despair over the amount of money he was losing because she wasn't cooperating. He was doing the two-step on the side of the stage in yet another attempt to get her to sing something a bit more snappy.

She ignored him and continued to work the crowd into a frenzy of regret. One man called out in a weepy shout to please sing that pretty song about his mama once again. Steeple frantically shook his head at Genevieve, but she simply couldn't refuse the request and launched into the heart-wrenching song one more time.

When she finished, they clapped and they wept, and Harry Steeple burst into tears.

Her throat was getting parched, and she decided to sing one last song and then take her leave. She poured her heart and her soul into the sweet, uplifting spiritual. It had always been a favorite of her father's, and her audience responded to the melody and the lyrics in much the same way he had. They stomped their feet and clapped their hands to the beat.

She was just reaching the high note in the last verse when she happened to notice the doors of the saloon open. Three men squeezed their way inside.

One of them was Ezekiel Jones.

She froze. She stopped singing so abruptly it was as though her voice had been cut off in mid-note by a blade. She jerked back, her gaze locked on Ezekiel, and she went completely rigid. She was staring into the glowing eyes of the devil himself, but she couldn't turn away, couldn't move, for what seemed an eternity. Fear immobilized her. Her hands balled into fists at her sides, and she could only stand there and watch as Ezekiel slowly threaded his way through the crowd. She kept telling herself to run, run, and finally the frantic thought penetrated her stupor and she turned to Adam and started to run to him, but just as suddenly she stopped.

He saw the panic in her eyes, took a step toward her, and at the same time swung his rifle up and scanned the audience looking for the threat.

She shook her head. No, she couldn't go to him. She wouldn't put him in such jeopardy. The jackals were closing in on her, and he would try to protect her. She couldn't risk Adam getting hurt, and she knew without a doubt that Ezekiel was capable of killing him.

Shuddering heavily, she turned toward Steeple and ran. Her hat flew down to the stage behind her. Steeple tried to grab her as she passed him, but she was too quick and he was too surprised by her abrupt departure.

Her satchel was on the chair next to the storage closet. She scooped it up in her arms as she raced by. She went out the back door into the alley, turned one way and then the other as she tried to remember which direction to take to the livery stable.

Adam was tearing the door open when she made up her mind and ran. He shouted her name and knew she heard him because she hesitated before she turned and disappeared around the corner. She was headed for the main street, and he was pretty certain she was going to the livery stable to get her horse and leave town.

He started to go after her, but just as he was about to reach the mouth of the alley, he heard the telltale squeak of the saloon's back door, and he quickly moved into the shadows behind a stack of crates.

Someone in that crowd had terrified her, and he was determined to find out who and why. He wasn't concerned that Genevieve would get away from him, because even if she did leave town, she would be easy to track in the moonlight.

His patience was quickly rewarded. Three of the homeliest and meanest-looking men he'd ever laid eyes on came strutting past. Two of them were big and bulky, and it soon became apparent that they took their orders from the shorter, heavier man dressed like a statesman at a funeral who trailed behind them.

Adam guessed the thugs were in the dandy's employ. When the man stopped at the entrance of the alley to strike a match to a cigar, the other two also stopped to wait for him.

"Do you want me to chase her down for you, Reverend?" the tallest of the three asked.

"No need to rush," the reverend answered in an accent that was as thick as southern maple syrup.

"The bitch won't be getting away from me this time," he crooned. "I've got her now, praise the Lord. I told you, Herman, that God would show me the way. Didn't I?"

"Yes, Reverend, you told me," Herman agreed.

He moved into the moonlight, and Adam got a good look at Herman's face. His forehead bulged out over his brows, his nose was crooked, no doubt from being broken a time or two, and there were scars on his cheeks that Adam thought were the result of a few knife fights. He looked exactly like what he was, a thug, and so did his companion.

"What do you want Lewis and me to do if she refuses to go back with you?" Herman asked.

Before the reverend could answer the question, Lewis stepped forward. "Will you want us to hurt her?" he asked eagerly.

"I expect so," the reverend crooned.

He motioned for his two companions to get out of his way and then walked into the street. "Come along, boys. God helps those who help themselves."

Adam had heard enough. He quietly followed the three men past the saloon and the hotel, but then he turned and took a shortcut between the buildings and shortened the distance to the livery stable by more than half.

He slipped inside without making a sound and bolted the doors behind him. He heard Genevieve before he saw her. She was whimpering low in her throat as she tried to swing the saddle up on her mare.

"Going somewhere?" he drawled out.

She jumped a foot and let out a loud yelp. She whirled around and found him standing right behind her inside the stall.

She felt as if her heart were going to explode. "You scared me."

"You were already scared."

He gently pushed her out of his way and took over the task of saddling her mare. He worked quickly and quietly. She picked up her bedroll and cradled it in her arms while she waited for him to demand an explanation.

He didn't say a word. He turned to her when he was finished, saw the bedroll, and suggested she leave it behind.

"Good God, no," she cried out.

He didn't have time to get into an argument with her. "Then tie it up behind the saddle."

He went into the adjacent stall and quickly saddled his stallion. She followed him and stood by his side, with her bedroll still in her arms.

"You can't go with me," she told him in no uncertain terms.

"Sure I can," he replied. There was a hard edge in his voice, indicating to her that he planned to be stubborn about it.

"Please listen to me. You can't go with me now. You could get hurt."

"What about you?"

"I don't want you to come with me."

"Too bad."

"Adam, please. I'm begging you. Walk away now."

"No," he snapped. "We're staying together. I'm

kind of anxious to get going. I just can't wait to get you alone for a few minutes so you can tell me again how you don't have any problems at all. Isn't that what you told me, Genevieve?"

She bowed her head. "I know you're angry with me."

"No, I'm not angry," he replied. "I've gone way past anger."

She started to say something more to him, but he put his hand up in a signal to be silent. Someone was pushing hard on the outer doors. Genevieve was turning toward the sound when Adam reached out and grabbed her. He wasn't gentle as he shoved her behind him and pushed her into the corner of the stall. He grabbed his rifle, cocked it, and then waited.

The doors crashed open, and Herman came running into the stable. Lewis was right behind him. The two men spread out to the opposite sides of the barn and squinted into the shadows.

Ezekiel Jones sauntered inside.

"My, my, it's dark in here. Where are you hiding, girl? I know you're in here. Maybe I ought to light the lantern and have a little look-see. I always liked to play hide-and-seek when I was a lad."

Adam could feel Genevieve trembling. She was also trying to get around him, but he made it impossible by squeezing her further into the corner. He was determined to protect her, even if she didn't want him to, and when she begged him in a whisper to save himself, he shook his head. He didn't dare turn to her, for it was imperative that he keep track of Ezekiel's two companions, who were slowly and methodically checking each stall as they made their way down the aisle.

They were getting closer. Ezekiel waited near the door. "Come out, come out, wherever you are," he called out in a singsong voice.

"Are you scared, girl? You ought to be scared. No one crosses Ezekiel Jones without suffering God's wrath."

"We need some light in here," Lewis called.

Ezekiel struck a match. The sizzling powder sounded like an explosion in the sudden silence. He lit a lantern and left it swaying back and forth on its hook, and then turned and shut the barn doors behind him.

"I wouldn't want any company coming inside to bother us," he drawled out. "And I wouldn't want you to get past me again, Miss Genevieve. There aren't any windows here to climb out, are there?"

Herman had steadily crept forward into the stall next to them and suddenly popped up. He was eye to eye with Genevieve. She didn't have time to shout a warning, but one wasn't necessary. Adam saw him at the same instant she did. He proved to be much quicker than the other man too. He used the butt of his rifle and struck him hard on the side of his head. Herman looked stupefied, and then his eyes rolled back into his head and he dropped down hard to the floor.

The noise brought Lewis running. He stopped short as soon as he saw the rifle pointed at him.

Ezekiel took his time strolling down the aisle to stand beside his hired gunman. His expression hardened when he spotted Adam, but just as quickly as his scowl appeared, it was replaced by a smile.

"Who are you, mister?"

"No one you need to know," Adam answered.

"I've got business with the woman you've got behind your back, but I don't have any quarrel with you. If you'll hand her over to me, you can leave, and no harm will come to you."

"I'm not going anywhere, and you're not getting near her."

"I'll make it worth your while."

"No."

There was pure hatred in Ezekiel's gaze as he stared at Adam. His voice lost its gentlemanly tone when he next spoke. "You're harboring a criminal and a sinner. She pulled you into her web of deceit, didn't she?"

Genevieve edged her way to Adam's side. "You're the criminal, not me," she cried out.

He pointed a finger at her. "Jezebel," he shouted.

"Just who the hell are you?" Adam demanded. "And what do you want with Genevieve?"

Ezekiel puffed up like a rooster. He held the lapel of his jacket with one hand and stood poised as though he were having his portrait done.

"I am the Reverend Ezekiel Jones," he announced importantly. "And she has something that belongs to me."

"I don't have anything that belongs to you."

"God will smite you for lying, girl."

"How dare you call yourself a preacher. You're nothing but a petty thief."

"My dear, there isn't anything remotely petty about me."

He looked at Adam again, feigned an expression of remorse, and said, "Like the sainted Paul, I too was a sinner before I was shown the light. I want my money back," he added in a snarl.

"I don't have your money," she cried out.

Lewis took a step forward. Adam fired into the ground in front of him. Dust flew up into his face, and he jumped back and very nearly knocked Ezekiel off his feet.

The reverend shoved him aside. "She took over four thousand dollars from me."

"No," she insisted. "I didn't take any of your money."

"She's lying," Ezekiel roared.

"Adam, you believe me, don't you?"

"You heard the lady. If she says she didn't take it, then she didn't. Now get out of here before I lose my patience and put a bullet in your pompous backside."

Ezekiel stood his ground. "Can't you see how she's blinded you to the truth? She's a jezebel, I tell you, and she'll take you to hell with her if you don't listen to me."

"Why don't we bring in the law and let the sheriff decide who's telling the truth," Adam suggested.

"No," Ezekiel blurted out. "There isn't any need to involve the law."

"Is that so?" Adam said.

"My checkered past still haunts me," Ezekiel confessed. He was trying hard to look contrite and failing miserably. "Otherwise, I'd run to get the sheriff. As God is my witness, I would."

"Get out of here," Adam ordered.

Ezekiel turned away. "This isn't over," he hissed.

Lewis tried to go to his friend, who was still unconscious on the floor in the next stall, but Adam wouldn't let him.

"Leave him be and get out," he ordered.

Ezekiel opened the barn door. "I'll get you, girl," he bellowed. "I know where you're headed, and I'm telling you now, you're never going to get there. Judgment Day is at hand."

And then he disappeared into the darkness. Lewis chased after him.

Genevieve fell back against the wall in exhaustion and relief.

Adam wouldn't let her relax. "We have to get out of here before they figure out how easy it would be to ambush us. Hurry, Genevieve. Ah, hell, now what are you doing?"

She had thrown herself into his arms and burst into tears. "Thank you for believing me."

He allowed himself a moment to hold her. He

squeezed her tight, bent down, and kissed her forehead. Then he pulled away.

"Let's go, sweetheart."

She wiped the tears away from her face with the back of her hands and stood there smiling up at him with a dazed look in her eyes.

"Now what?" he asked gruffly.

"You called me sweetheart."

"Yes, I did," he said. "Now move it."

He tried to lift her up into the saddle. She backed away. "My bedroll," she explained.

She turned around and picked it up from the corner of the stall where she'd dropped it, but Adam was quicker. He grabbed one end and swung the bedroll up behind the saddle.

Then he froze and watched in disbelief as a hundred-dollar bill slowly floated down from the bedroll to the floor. It landed between his feet.

He stared at it for several seconds and then bent down to pick it up. He didn't say a word to her, and his expression showed only mild curiosity as he turned to look at the bedroll again. Before she realized what he was going to do, he untied the rope holding the bedroll secure and then flipped it open in front of him.

Hundreds of bills poured down like rain on his feet until he was standing in a pyramid of money. He was pretty certain he knew how much was there, but he decided to find out the exact amount anyway.

His gaze slowly moved to hers. "Four thousand?" he asked quietly.

She shook her head. "Close to five," she said. "Four thousand seven hundred and three dollars, to be exact."

"Ezekiel's money, I assume." His voice blazed with anger.

He was so furious with her he could barely speak,

yet he couldn't help but notice she didn't look the least bit guilty or contrite. She didn't appear to be at all worried either.

"Care to explain, Genevieve?"

She folded her arms across her waist. "I didn't steal Ezekiel's money."

He glanced down at the pile and back up at her. The evidence was damning.

"Adam?"

"What?"

"You *will* believe me."

Ten

❧

From the moment he'd met her, she'd done nothing but lie—or so it seemed—and there was absolutely no reason to believe she was telling the truth now. And yet he did believe her. He was either the most gullible man in the world or just plumb crazy. Regardless, he trusted her.

She wasn't a thief. Therefore, there had to be a logical explanation for why she just happened to have all that money with her, and just as soon as possible, he was going to sit her down and demand that she tell him everything.

He didn't speak to her again until they made camp about twelve miles south of Gramby. He asked her to get a fire started while he backtracked to find out if they were being followed. By the time he returned to the campsite, she had the bedrolls laid out and a pot of coffee brewing over the flames.

She waited until after he had taken care of the horses and had eaten his supper to bring up the topic she was sure would give him indigestion.

"I don't think it's a good idea to keep the money in my satchel, because that's the first place Ezekiel will look for it."

"Hopefully he won't get close enough to look."

He glanced around the campsite. He remembered dropping the satchel next to the bedrolls, but it wasn't there now.

"What'd you do with the money?"

She pointed to a jagged boulder about twenty feet away from where she was seated. "I hid the satchel behind that rock under some bushes."

He dropped down beside her and added some twigs to the fire. She offered him an apple, and when he shook his head, she put it back in her lap.

"Could you tell if Ezekiel was following us or not?"

"No," he replied. "The clouds were already moving in. If he is, he's going to have a hell of a time seeing our tracks."

"Won't he see the smoke from our fire?"

"With all this mist? No, he won't see it."

"Why is it so damp here?"

"We're close to Juniper Falls," he replied. "Genevieve, what could you have been thinking, carrying all that money? My God, you left it in the stable with the horses."

"No one ever steals an old bedroll," she said. "It was safer there than in the saloon."

He was trying to keep his temper under control. "I think you'd better start explaining. If you didn't steal the money from Ezekiel, then where did you get it?"

"Oh, I stole the money from him all right."

His mouth dropped open. "You what?"

She put her hand on his knee in an attempt to calm him. "Don't get mad until you've heard everything. I did take the money from Ezekiel, but it never belonged to him. I guess you could say I stole from a thief. Yes, that's exactly what I did," she added with a nod.

"Start at the beginning and try to make sense."

"I just hate it when you snap orders at me like that."

"Start talking, Genevieve."

His impatience irritated her. She put the apple back in the burlap sack and folded her hands in her lap.

"I was duped, just like everyone else. I remember telling you that I attended the same church your mother had joined and that I sang in the choir," she said. "Once a year, on Palm Sunday, an assembly of preachers would join the congregation and one would be chosen by our preacher to give the sermon. On one such occasion, the Reverend Thomas Kerriman spoke. He was begging for our help and told us that he was going to lead a large group of families to Kansas to join a settlement there. The families were in a hard way, Adam. They didn't have money or clothes or food, but what they did have was a will to start over again and build a new life. Reverend Kerriman was their Moses."

"And was he like Ezekiel Jones?"

"Oh, no, he's the complete opposite. I knew Thomas before he became a preacher. We grew up together in the same parish, and I know for a fact that he's a good and decent man. He would never dupe anyone."

"So what happened?"

"Ezekiel was also in the congregation that day. He stepped forward and promised Kerriman that he had a sure way to help him. He pointed to the choir and said that if the members agreed, he would take us from town to town to sing, and all the donations would go to Kerriman's cause. He singled me out and said that my voice alone would guarantee large donations." She sounded ashamed.

"You have a beautiful voice, Genevieve," Adam remarked.

"Thank you," she replied. "My father used to tell me that God gives each one of us a special talent and it's up to us to decide if we will use that talent for good or evil. I didn't understand at the time what he meant. I do now."

"Because of Ezekiel?"

"No, because of me. I let him turn my head with all his compliments. I liked being singled out, Adam, and I started dreaming about fame and fortune. He easily drew me into his scheme. I was very full of myself back then, and Ezekiel fed my pride. I'm very ashamed of the person I became. I acted like a spoiled child," she added. "Fame went to my head, and before long the only friend I had left in the choir was Lottie."

"The woman who sent you the wire."

"Yes," she replied.

"So you went from town to town singing and collecting money."

"Yes," she said. "Ezekiel became more and more demanding. I was never allowed to go anywhere by myself or with my friend. He hired men to watch over me . . ."

"Lewis and Herman?"

She nodded. "Ezekiel told me they were there to protect me, but I was more afraid of them than the men they were protecting me from. I still stubbornly clung to my dream of being famous, and then something happened and I saw how shallow and empty my life was becoming."

"What happened?"

"My mother died and I didn't even know about it until two weeks after her funeral. We were singing in Birmingham, and one of her friends come all that way to tell me. I found out later that she had sent a wire to Ezekiel when my mother became ill, but he hid it from me. I will never forgive myself or him."

"If you didn't know—"

"I should have known," she whispered. "I should have gone home more often to see her, but I was so caught up in my own dreams I forgot what was the most important thing of all."

"Family."

"Yes, family."

"Would Ezekiel have let you leave?"

"No, but I could have found a way."

He put his arm around her shoulders and pulled her into his side. "What about your father?"

"He died a year before my mother."

He let out a sigh. "I understand why you want to go to Paris. Your grandfather's the only family left, isn't he?"

"I didn't exactly tell you the truth about my grandfather. He is in Paris . . ."

"But?"

"He died a long time ago. I'm going there to pay my respects."

"Why did you let me think he was alive?"

She glanced over at him. "If you had thought I was all alone in the world, you would have felt sorry for me, and I didn't want that to happen."

The tenderness in his eyes made her want to curl up in his lap and cling to him. She turned away, resisting the lure, and said, "Lots of people are alone, so stop looking at me like that. Now, do you want to hear the rest of this or not?"

"Yes, I want to hear the rest of it."

He was gently rubbing her arm. She never wanted him to stop, and as soon as that thought came into her mind, she pushed his hand away.

"When I heard my mother had died, I wanted to go home, and that's when Ezekiel started locking me in my room. I heard him tell Lewis I was his meal ticket. It was a horrible time. The shock of losing my mother put everything in perspective. I knew I was chasing a fool's dream and didn't want fame or fortune. I kept thinking about my father and what he'd told me. I could use my talent for good or bad. The choice was up to me. I made up my mind that I would only sing for money when it was absolutely necessary."

"You sang for money in the saloon."

"Yes, but I did so out of necessity, not vanity, and I only sang hymns. We needed money for food and shelter."

"You have almost five thousand dollars," he reminded her.

"But that isn't my money. It belongs to Reverend Kerriman and his families."

He nodded to let her know he understood. "Tell me how you managed to get the money away from Ezekiel."

"One afternoon when we were in New Orleans I was sitting in the garden of a lovely old church and I happened to see Thomas in the courtyard. He was talking to Ezekiel, and I could see how upset he was. Ezekiel wasn't upset though. He was laughing and mocking Thomas."

"Where was your guard?"

"Lewis was assigned to me that day. I let him lock me in my room, and then I snuck out."

"Through the window."

"Yes, I went out through the window and ran back to the courtyard. I heard Ezekiel boast that he had collected over four thousand dollars and that he wasn't going to give Thomas one cent."

"And what did Thomas do?"

"He threatened to go to the authorities, and Ezekiel went into a rage. He told him he'd kill him if he said a word to anyone. Thomas didn't believe him at first, but Ezekiel told him he'd killed before and he could kill again.

"Lewis and Herman started beating Thomas. He fell to the ground, and then Ezekiel kicked him over and over again. I was so terrified for him I couldn't even scream. I ran toward him to make them stop pounding him, but some other people got there first. Lewis and Herman ran. Ezekiel didn't run though. As arrogant as ever, he turned around and strolled back to the church."

"And that's when you decided to steal the money from him, isn't it?"

"Yes. I went to his room and found it right away under his mattress. The stupid man slept on it every night. I put it in a satchel, and then I left."

"To go to Rosehill?"

She shook her head. "Thomas was taken to the hospital, and I hid in New Orleans and waited for him to recover so I could give him the money. I didn't dare go and visit him because I was afraid of being spotted by Ezekiel's men, and when I finally got up enough courage to sneak in during the night, I found out he'd already left for Kansas."

"And that's where you're headed now, isn't it?"

"Yes," she answered. "When I left New Orleans, I was going to go directly to the settlement in Kansas, but then I started worrying about Ezekiel. He knew I had seen what he and his men had done to Thomas, and he had to have figured out why I took the money. I was afraid he would follow me, and I didn't like the idea of being ambushed along the way."

"So you came to Rosehill."

"I thought the ranch was a perfect place to hide for a little while, and I was so sure Ezekiel wouldn't follow me there."

"I wish to God you had told me all of this when we were in the library together."

"I didn't want you to get involved. It was my problem, and I had to take care of it. If I had confided in you, you would have insisted on taking the money to Thomas for me, which would have put you in danger. Isn't that so?"

"Yes," he agreed.

"I don't want anyone else to give Thomas the money. It's important to me that he know I wasn't involved in Ezekiel's scheme."

"I'm sure he already knows that."

"I also want to tell him how sorry I am, but I have to be realistic. Ezekiel isn't going to give up, is he?"

"No, he isn't," he said. "Five thousand dollars is worth his trouble."

"Will you promise me something?" She pushed his arm away and turned to face him. "If anything happens to me, or if we should get separated, will you take the money to Thomas?"

"I'm not going to let anything happen to you."

"Adam, the money's important to those people. It will buy food and clothes and peace of mind. Promise me," she demanded.

"I promise."

She bowed her head. "I can't imagine what you must think of me. I was so naive and stupid and vain and . . ."

He stopped her from berating herself by tilting her chin up and kissing her. His mouth brushed over hers in a gentle, undemanding caress.

"You're good-hearted," he whispered gruffly.

She pulled back. "I can't let you think that. I'm not good-hearted. If I hadn't been so full of myself, I would have seen through Ezekiel right away. I acted like a fool, but I've learned my lesson. Now do you understand why I've become so cynical?"

Because she was being so earnest, he didn't dare laugh. He couldn't contain his smile though. "I understand you might want to be cynical, but, sweetheart, you haven't quite mastered it yet. There isn't anything cynical about you. You're one of the most trusting souls I've ever met. You have a beautiful heart, Genevieve."

"You did it again," she whispered.

He was slowly pulling her onto his lap. She didn't resist and, in fact, put her arms around his neck.

She stared into his eyes and thought that he was the most amazingly perfect man in the whole world. How would she ever have the strength to leave him?

"What did I do?" he asked.

"You called me sweetheart," she told him in a breathless whisper. "You mustn't do that anymore."

"Why not?"

"Because I like it," she stammered. "And now you're going to kiss me again, aren't you? And you really shouldn't. When the time comes for us to go our separate ways, it's going to be very difficult for me, and if you keep kissing me, I'll end up miserable. I have to go to Paris, and you have to go back home. We should just be friends, shouldn't we? But, Adam, I think I really want you to kiss me now. Just one, last kiss, and then we . . ."

"Shake hands?" he suggested dryly.

"Yes, or you could give me a peck on the cheek, the way friends do."

She wanted friendship and nothing more? Didn't she understand they had gone way past that stage? Maybe it was his fault, he decided. He hadn't told her how he felt about her. He hadn't allowed himself to think about it, much less discuss it. He knew he cared for her, but as he did with everything else, he wanted to think about all the ramifications before he told her.

His voice was deceptively mild when he said, "I think you need to get something straight in your head. I don't kiss my friends, I don't peck my friends, and I sure as certain don't call my friends sweetheart."

"We can't become involved."

She really was an exasperating woman. "We *are* involved."

She looked miserable. "We're all wrong for each

other. You do realize that, don't you? You want peace and quiet. I'm a troublemaker."

"No, you're not. You're aggravating and as stubborn as can be, but you aren't a troublemaker, and I'm definitely not your friend."

She was slowly pulling back from him. He wasn't about to let her get away. He jerked her hard against his chest, ignoring her startled cry of surprise. His hand cupped the back of her head, and as he was moving toward her, he whispered, "I never had a chance, did I?"

She didn't understand what he meant, and he was too busy kissing her to explain.

His mouth was warm and firm against hers. It wasn't a friendly kiss. He made sure of that. He coaxed her mouth open, and his tongue swept inside to mate with hers. She began to respond, timidly at first and then with growing passion. He melted away her inhibitions in a matter of heartbeats, and, Lord, she tasted as sweet and fresh as he remembered. He couldn't get enough of her. Passion flowed between them as his mouth slanted over hers again and again, and when at last he forced himself to pull back, he couldn't seem to draw a proper breath. Her own shortness of breath was music to his ears.

The hell he was her friend.

"Now do you want to shake my hand?" he asked, driving his point home.

His sarcasm was lost on her. She was blissfully content snuggled up against him. Her head rested in the crook of his neck and her eyes closed in sweet surrender to the moment.

He held her for a long while in his arms. His hands tenderly caressed her back, and all he wanted to think about was her soft body. Unfortunately, thoughts of Ezekiel Jones kept intruding.

"What are you thinking about?"

"Ezekiel Jones," he said.

"I knew it had to be something unpleasant. You're squeezing the breath out of me, and your muscles have become rigid."

He forced himself to relax and loosened his grip on her. "Is that better?"

"Yes," she answered. "I should probably get off your lap, but I don't want to move," she admitted. "I was also thinking about Ezekiel. Do you think he was telling the truth when he said he had gotten away with murder? Or was he just trying to scare us?"

"I think he was telling the truth, and I'd sure be interested in finding out the particulars. You told me Ezekiel changed his name. Do you know what his real name is?"

"Henry Stevens," she answered. "I heard Lewis call him by his full name once. Ezekiel became furious and threatened dire consequences if he ever called him by his real name again. The stupid man was yelling so loud most of the choir heard him."

Adam filed the information away. Henry Stevens. He wouldn't forget the name again. Had Ezekiel changed his name because he was a wanted man, or had the crime gone unreported? Adam decided to find out as soon as possible.

"When we get to Salt Lake City, I think I'd like to pay a visit to the marshal's office."

"I doubt anyone's there. Don't you remember Mr. Steeple told us that three U.S. marshals were in Middleton, investigating the bank robbery?"

The plan came to him all of a sudden, and he found himself smiling in anticipation. His idea was perfect, and if it worked, it would be well worth the risk. Ezekiel would get what was coming to him, and Adam wouldn't have to kill him. There were a lot of *ifs* involved. If he could find a safe place for Genevieve, and if he could trick Ezekiel into following him to

Middleton, and if the marshals were indeed there, then Adam would lead the bastard right into their hands.

"I think we should split up," she said.

She'd spoken his thought aloud. "Is that so?" he asked.

"Yes," she said. "One of us should lead Ezekiel north, while the other takes the money to Kansas."

He shook his head. "The money should go in a bank until I've dealt with Ezekiel and his friends."

"Are you crazy? There are bank robbers roaming these hills. They'll steal it. My plan makes sense."

"I've got a better plan. We'll find a safe place for you, and I'll take care of Ezekiel."

"It's out of the question. This is my problem and I have to solve it."

"No, it's our problem, but I'm going to solve it. You aren't going with me. I would be worried about you the entire time, and I wouldn't be able to concentrate on what I needed to do."

"Such as?"

"Putting an end to Ezekiel's terror tactics."

"It's very sweet of you to be worried about me, but, Adam, I won't be left out. Do you expect me to sit quietly in a parlor somewhere while you put yourself in such danger? I won't hear of it."

He smiled. "I wasn't thinking of putting you in a parlor. I have another place in mind where I can be absolutely certain Ezekiel won't go near you or the money."

"There isn't any such place."

He kissed her again just to get her to stop arguing with him. "Trust me, Genevieve. I've thought of the perfect place."

Eleven

$\mathcal{H}$e put her in jail. Even though she had to admit it was a perfect place to keep the money safe, she still wasn't happy about Adam's choice, because she knew he expected her to stay inside while he went gallivanting after Ezekiel and his men. If she had had a few minutes alone with him, she would have let him know just how unhappy she was, but the jail was crowded with lawmen, and she wasn't about to criticize Adam in front of strangers. She did glare at him though when he suggested she might be more comfortable inside one of the empty cells.

She sat down in a chair next to Sheriff Norton's desk, put her satchel on her lap, and folded her hands on top. Adam stood behind her. After removing a stack of papers from his chair, the sheriff sat down and tilted back against the wall. He was an older man with a big belly and melancholy eyes. His face reminded Genevieve of a hound dog's. His jowls extended past his chin, and when he smiled—which seemed to be most of the time—the folds of extra skin on either side of his face wrinkled up to his ears. He was very kind to her and Adam, and she liked him immensely. His voice radiated fatherly concern when he asked how he could be of help, and he listened patiently without interrupting once while Adam explained why they were there.

Two U.S. marshals leaned against the wall and listened. The men were so similar in appearance and attitude they could have been brothers. They were about the same height, nearly six feet, and had the same worn and world-weary expressions. The more muscular one was named Davidson, and the other was called Morgan.

Their presence should have been a comfort, but they made her nervous instead. Their gazes seemed to bore right through her. There was an air of danger about them as well. She couldn't even begin to imagine the horrors they must have seen that would have turned them into such frightening men. Her mind conjured up one horrible possibility after another, and before long she was fighting the urge to jump up and leave.

She really wished they would stop staring at her. She kept expecting one of them to pounce on her, and she glanced over at them every other minute just to make sure they hadn't moved.

Adam must have sensed her unease because he put his hand on her shoulder and gave it a little squeeze.

After he had finished explaining their circumstances to the sheriff, including details she wished he hadn't mentioned, Marshal Davidson suggested that Genevieve look through the posters of wanted men to see if Ezekiel was one of them.

The sheriff pointed to a knee-high stack of papers on the floor in the corner behind him. "There they are, but I'll wager you it will take you the rest of the day to sort through them."

"Adam, are you certain Jones and his friends are following you?" Morgan asked the question but watched Genevieve all the while.

"Yes, I made sure they could easily follow my tracks to Middleton."

Davidson took a step toward her. She visibly jumped and then became angry.

"Gentlemen, what are you staring at?" she demanded.

The marshals glanced at one another before turning back to her. Davidson raised an eyebrow and looked a little sheepish, but Morgan maintained his glacial expression. She didn't think the man had blinked in the past five minutes.

"I was looking at you, ma'am," Davidson said.

"I wish you wouldn't," she said. "I swear to heaven you make me want to confess to a crime just to get you to stop."

"Did you have a particular crime in mind?" Morgan asked. A hint of a smile crinkled the corners of his eyes.

The marshal became human to her. She began to relax. "No," she answered. "I would have to make one up. Do you know how intimidating you are? Yes, of course you do. That's how you interrogate criminals, isn't it?"

"Genevieve, what are you talking about?" Adam asked.

"You wouldn't understand even if I tried to explain. You do the very same thing."

Davidson burst into laughter. "Ma'am, did you really impersonate Ruby Leigh . . . ?"

"Diamond," Morgan supplied with a grin.

"You sure don't look like the kind of woman who would go by such a name," Davidson remarked.

She frowned at the marshal. "How exactly do I look?"

"Refined," Davidson answered. "You're a lady, and I'm having trouble picturing you up on a stage in a saloon."

"I didn't impersonate anyone, at least not on purpose. Mr. Steeple tricked me. Adam, you really didn't need to tell the marshals I sang in a saloon."

He squeezed her shoulder again. Davidson came to his defense. "He was telling us how he first spotted Ezekiel, so he had to mention the saloon."

"I assure you I'm not in the habit of entertaining drunken men, and I only sang church songs."

"Did you really make all of those men cry?" Morgan asked.

"Not on purpose."

Her answer made them laugh again. Her embarrassment intensified. She waited until the noise died down before suggesting in a righteous stammer that they tell her what they were going to do about Ezekiel and his friends.

Norton reached over to pat her hand. "Don't you be worrying about it, little lady."

His condescending tone of voice didn't sit well with her. "Sheriff, Ezekiel Jones is coming after me. I have to be worried about him, and I also have to be worried about Adam. He's determined to go after all three of those horrible men. Please stop squeezing my shoulder," she added with a quick glance up at Adam. "I don't want you to get hurt."

"My mind's made up," he told her in no uncertain terms.

She turned back to the marshals. "Well?" she demanded.

"Well, what?" Davidson asked.

"I'm waiting for one of you to tell Adam he can't take the law into his own hands."

Morgan shrugged. His response wasn't what she was hoping for. Neither was his reply. "He seems real determined, ma'am, and I don't think anything I say will change his mind. I don't blame him for wanting to go after Jones. If the woman I loved were being threatened, I sure as certain would put a stop to it."

She didn't know if she should correct the marshal's assumption or not. Adam didn't love her; he was simply being compassionate by helping her. That was all.

"If Ezekiel's wanted for murder or any other crime, I'd be real interested in talking to him," Morgan continued.

The marshal's casual attitude drove her to distraction. "I don't want you to talk to him. I want you to lock him up. If the murder he committed wasn't reported, then I shall press charges against him."

"On what grounds?" the sheriff asked.

"The man locked me in my room."

"Begging your pardon, but it's your word against his, and I don't think he's gonna admit locking you up," the sheriff told her.

"The sooner you go through the posters, the better," Davidson suggested.

"Yes, of course, but in the meanwhile, I want you to arrest Ezekiel and his two friends. I'll be happy to give you their descriptions."

"Now we're right back where we started," the sheriff complained. "As I was telling you before, you just got to have grounds to make an arrest."

"Such as?" she asked.

The sheriff pondered the question a long minute before answering. "If one of them happens to take a shot at you, well then, we could nab him for attempted murder."

Davidson grinned. "I know it's frustrating, ma'am, but the law's the law. Maybe we could talk to him and scare him into leaving you alone."

"We ought to ask Ryan to have a word with Ezekiel," Morgan told his friend.

"Adam, what do you think?" Genevieve asked.

She turned to look up at him and only then discovered he was gone. "When did he leave?"

She was on her feet and turning toward the door before the sheriff could answer her.

"He took off a few minutes ago," he said. "Sit back down, ma'am. You got to start looking through the posters. These here are the latest ones, but if you think Jones might have committed a crime a while back, then I got to take you into the storeroom. I keep every poster I receive. Some go back as far as ten years."

"While you're looking through them, Morgan and I will stop by the telegraph office and send a couple of wires asking for information. Adam gave us a good description, and we should hear something back real soon. In the meantime, you're in good hands," Davidson said.

"Are you boys headed back up the mountain?"

Morgan nodded. "Ryan's going to stick close to the doctor's house as long as there's a chance our witness will make it. If you run into any trouble, he'll lend a hand."

Genevieve watched the marshals leave and then turned to the sheriff and asked, "Mr. Steeple told me there were three marshals in Middleton. Ryan's the third one, isn't he?"

"Yes, ma'am. Morgan and Davidson are taking orders from him, and I heard Morgan say Ryan was senior man in charge. He's also the youngest."

"Is Ryan's first name Daniel by any chance?"

"It sure is," he replied. "I don't expect I'll ever be calling him anything but marshal or sir. He ain't the type to get friendly with. Fact is, he scares just about everybody in town, and I imagine that's why Morgan suggested Ryan be the one to talk to Ezekiel Jones or Henry Stevens or whatever in tarnation his name is."

"What did Morgan mean when he said that Marshal Ryan was staying close to the doctor's house?"

"He's over at Doc Garrison's house, waiting to see if poor old Luke MacFarland is gonna up and die on him. He's the only witness we got to the terrible trouble we had here the day before yesterday. What started out as a plain old bank robbery turned into a massacre. Luke was outside and saw what happened through the bank window. Before he passed out on us, he told Ryan and me he could identify the leader.

"The folks working at the bank handed the money over as meek as could be and then put their hands up to let the robbers know they weren't gonna be heroic and go for their guns. There weren't no call to shoot them down, no call at all, but that's what the robbers did. Frank Holden, the president of the bank, had six bullets in his head. There was blood splattered all the way up to the ceiling. It was a cold, vicious act, and five good men I called friends died like dogs."

Genevieve was sickened by the story. "Those poor souls," she whispered. "If they didn't put up a fight, why were they killed?"

"They would have been witnesses, that's why. Luke and Nichols were watching all of it. Both of them got shot. Luke took a bullet in his gut, and that means he don't have much hope of lasting, which is a crying shame for his family. He's got a wife and four boys to feed, and if he dies, I don't know what will happen to them."

"What about the other witness?" she asked.

"Nichols took a bullet through his heart. Doc said he probably died standing up."

"I hope the marshals catch the men and lock them up for the rest of their lives."

"I'd rather they strung them up," Norton said. "You can understand now, can't you, why Davidson and Morgan are letting Adam take care of Ezekiel? They got their hands full trailing the gang. None of the marshals have had much sleep lately."

"Do you think they'll find the gang?"

"Maybe, and maybe not. There's over a hundred caves in these mountains, and they could be hiding out in any one of them. Eventually they'll get caught because they're bound to make a mistake. The five of them have been on a killing spree for over a year now. The man in charge is a clever devil to be able to elude Ryan for so long. The bastard always makes sure there ain't no witnesses, just in case he gets caught."

The sheriff stood up and stretched his arms wide. "If you don't mind being alone, I'd like to go over to the doc's house and see how Luke's doing."

"I don't mind," she replied. "But if you happen to run into Adam, will you please tell him I'd like him to help me go through the posters?"

"I doubt I'll see him anytime soon," the sheriff responded. "We both know he went looking for those fellas. Why, he's probably waiting by the hill outside of town. That's what I'd do if I wanted to nab someone coming from Gramby. The only way into Middleton is over that hill beyond the stable. I got a feeling he'll come back empty-handed by nightfall, 'cause if you heard there were three marshals here, this Jones fella probably heard the same thing."

Genevieve shook her head. "I don't think Ezekiel was in town long enough to talk to anyone. At least that's what Adam hopes. Sheriff, I'm worried about him. Ezekiel is terribly bold, and the two men riding with him wouldn't think twice about shooting a man in the back."

"I don't want you sitting in here fretting," the sheriff told her. "Maybe I will mosey on up the hill and have a look around for Adam. He probably don't need my help though. From the looks of him, I'd say he could hold his own in any fight, even against three."

He showed her where the storeroom was located and then left her alone. At first sight, she thought the task was hopeless, for there were papers stacked everywhere. They lined the shelves to the ceiling, and more were on the floor. The dust made her sneeze, and some of the old posters crumbled when she touched them.

It wasn't as chaotic as she'd first thought though. The sheriff had separated the posters by the year they were received. She ignored the latest notices and, starting with the year-old fliers, worked her way back.

After three hours of searching, she was stiff from sitting on the floor, hungry, and covered with dust. When she stretched her legs out to get rid of a cramp in her calf, she knocked over a pile of posters she had yet to look through. With a sigh, she leaned forward to straighten them up, and then let out a whoop of joy. Ezekiel Jones's ugly face was staring up at her.

The drawing had done Ezekiel justice, because it captured the evil essence of the man right down to the detail of his beady, squinty eyes. He was wanted for murder and extortion, he was considered armed and dangerous—and she could certainly testify to those two facts—and there was a hundred-dollar reward for his apprehension. Several of the aliases he had used were listed at the bottom of the sheet, and in bold letters across the top was the notice that he was wanted dead or alive.

She was so excited with her discovery she could barely think what to do. Adam needed to see the poster as soon as possible. Surely then he would realize what a dangerous adversary he was up against. My God, the man really had committed murder. She had heard him boast of the heinous crime, but a part of her hadn't believed him. The poster removed all doubt. Ezekiel was a killer. Hopefully, after Adam had seen the poster, he would agree to let the authorities take over the hunt.

She grabbed her satchel and hurried to the front door and then decided it was foolish to carry Thomas's money with her. She ran back to the jail cells and locked the satchel inside one of them. She wasn't about to leave the keys behind, and so she slipped the heavy metal ring over her wrist and wore it like a bracelet. The keys jingled and jangled with each step she took down the boardwalk.

The streets and the boardwalk were crowded with people coming and going. She wasn't quite sure where Adam was, but she hoped he was waiting for Ezekiel near the base of the hills behind the livery stable. The sheriff had told them that the main road from Gramby led into Middleton from the north, and if Ezekiel was coming after them, he would probably use that route. Earlier she had hoped that Ezekiel hadn't heard that U.S. marshals had converged on Middleton, but now she prayed he had indeed heard, so that he would stay away. The thought of Adam taking on not one but three blackguards frightened her. He played by the rules. He would never shoot a man in the back. Ezekiel would.

The possibility terrified her, and before she realized what she was doing, she started running down the boardwalk toward the livery.

A shot rang out. The noise so jarred her she stumbled. She grabbed hold of a hitching post to keep from falling and dropped the poster. She scooped it up, folded it, and shoved it in her pocket as she squinted into the sunlight to see who was firing his gun. Someone shouted to her, but the words were drowned out by a hail of gunfire. The noise was explosive, the sound ricocheting from building to building. The men and women who had been strolling down the main thoroughfare ran for cover, and within seconds, the streets and boardwalk were deserted.

She was frozen with panic. She saw a man running down the center of the street toward the sound, his gun drawn. He was moving so fast into the sunlight he was almost a blur.

A yellow-haired woman poked her head out of the general store a few feet in front of Genevieve and shouted to her. "Get on inside here before you get yourself killed."

"The gang who robbed the bank came back, and now we're all gonna die," another woman screeched from behind the first.

Genevieve turned to go inside. Then she stopped. Why would the robbers come back? They already had the money from the bank. What if it wasn't the gang . . . ?

Adam. A chill went down her spine. Oh, God, what if Adam was in trouble? She had assumed he had gone in search of Ezekiel, but what if he had returned to town? She pictured him pinned down and surrounded by Lewis and Herman and Ezekiel, and, dear God, what if he had already been shot? She had to find out. She just needed to get close enough to see for herself that Adam wasn't involved.

She picked up her skirts and ran. The noise seemed to be coming from between two buildings on the next street. The sun was blinding her, and fear was making it hard to breathe. Panting, she raced forward as though his life depended on it. She was leaping off the boardwalk between the alley and the next building when she heard someone whisper her name. She stumbled as she turned to see who was there.

And then she screamed.

Twelve

He had them right where he wanted them. Adam pressed back against the brick wall facing the street and quickly reloaded his gun. He was on the left side of the entrance to an alley that dead-ended, and he was feeling damned smug because he was certain he had all three of the bastards pinned inside.

His mood wasn't friendly. One of them had tried to ambush him behind the livery stable just as he had been dismounting, and if he hadn't thrown himself off his horse and to the ground in the nick of time, he would have taken a bullet in the back.

He wanted to get even, and though he fancied the notion of killing all of them, he knew he would have to settle for wounding one or two. It was his fervent hope that Ezekiel would become desperate enough to try to rush past him. There wasn't any other way out of the alley, and if Adam had to spend the rest of the day waiting to nab him, then that's what he would do.

He spotted a man running toward him from across the street. The stranger was wearing a badge, and

Adam assumed he was the third marshal he'd heard about. The lawman was tall, thick-shouldered, and had blond hair and blue eyes.

He seemed familiar, but Adam couldn't remember where he had seen him before. Adam nodded to him and was just turning away when he spotted a gold chain dangling from the marshal's vest pocket. What looked suspiciously like a gold compass case dangled from the end of the chain.

Recognition was immediate. "Son of a . . ." Adam whispered. The lawman was Daniel Ryan.

"Drop your gun," Ryan roared.

Adam shook his head and went right on reloading.

The marshal aimed his gun at him and was repeating his command when a shot rang out. The bullet roared past Ryan's left shoulder. He dove for cover on the opposite side of the entrance, and like Adam, pressed his back against the wall.

His gaze was directed on Adam. "Who the hell are they?" he roared.

Adam quickly explained. When he was finished, Ryan asked him how many there were.

"Ezekiel was leading the way and his two hired guns were following him. When I turned the corner, I saw one of them run into the alley. I'm certain all three are there. They must have thought they could cut through, and now they're trapped. When they run out of bullets, they'll come out."

Ryan nodded. "I'll handle this. Just stay out of my way."

"No," Adam answered. "You stay out of my way. You're Daniel Ryan, aren't you?"

"Yes. Who are you?"

"Adam Clayborne."

Ryan raised an eyebrow in surprise, and then a hint of a smile lifted the corners of his mouth. "You're Rose's son."

"Yes," Adam agreed. "Nice compass."

"Yes, it is."

"The compass belongs to my brother Cole."

"It sure does," Ryan agreed.

Before Adam could demand that he hand it over, Ryan shouted to the men in the alley. "Drop your weapons and put your hands up, or you're going to die."

A hail of bullets whizzed past in response. Ryan leaned in, shot twice, and then jerked back.

"How's your mother doing?" he asked in a voice as mild as the afternoon breeze.

"She's fine," Adam replied a scant second before he moved forward, took aim, and shot. One of the men let out a loud wail of distress.

The sound made Adam smile. He pressed back against the wall and grinned. "One down, two to go."

"Stay out of this."

"No way."

"What's Cole up to these days?"

"Ranching."

"You ready to give it up?" Ryan bellowed. "This is the last time I'm gonna ask you."

"Go to hell," one of the men shouted.

Ryan let out a sigh. "Seems like they want to die," he drawled out.

Adam nodded. "It seems so."

"Less paperwork involved," Ryan remarked. "So I might as well accommodate them."

"Ezekiel Jones is mine. If anyone's going to shoot him, it's going to be me."

Ryan shrugged. "Does Rose like living in Montana?"

"Yes, she does. She speaks highly of you, and she seems to think you're going to bring the compass you borrowed back to her," he added, deliberately stressing the word "borrowed."

Ryan laughed. "I didn't borrow it. I took it."

"Give it back."

"I will when I'm ready. I've got some business to discuss with Cole, and as soon as I've finished up here, I'm coming to Rosehill."

"You'd better come armed then. You've made Cole angry enough to shoot you on sight."

Ryan smiled. "He doesn't have a problem killing, does he?"

"No, none at all."

"Good. That's what I heard. He's just the man I need."

"Need? What do you need him for? You can't possibly think he'd go to work for you."

"That's exactly what I think. I can be real persuasive."

The conversation was interrupted by gunshots from the alley. Ryan and Adam returned the fire. The sound was deafening. Both men fell back against the wall and reloaded.

"What exactly do you want Cole to do for you?"

"Kill some vermin."

Before Adam could question him further, one of Ezekiel's men shouted at them.

"We're coming out. Don't shoot."

"Drop your weapons and put your hands up," Ryan shouted.

After giving the order, he motioned for Adam to stay where he was, and then Ryan moved back at an angle into the street.

Herman came strutting out of the alley first. He was closely followed by Lewis, who was limping. The two men had just reached the entrance when Lewis, using Herman as his shield, fired at Ryan and missed. The marshal shot the gun out of his hand a scant second before Adam slammed the butt of his gun up against the side of his head. Lewis crumpled to the ground.

In one fluid motion Herman dove for the ground

and reached behind his back for his weapon. He was swinging his arm up with a gun in his hand before he hit the ground.

Ryan shot to kill. The bullet sliced through Herman's chest, propelling him backward. He died before his head struck the edge of the boardwalk.

Adam moved into the alley to search for Ezekiel. The bastard wasn't there. Muttering curses under his breath, he reholstered his gun and turned around. Ryan had moved to the center of the street and was staring at something in front of him. He looked as though he was ready for a shoot-out. His legs were braced apart, his back was rigid, and his hand hovered just above the hilt of his gun.

"Let her go," Ryan shouted.

Adam ran forward, ignoring the signal the lawman gave him to stay where he was. Adam was about ten feet away from Ryan when he saw the two of them. Genevieve—his sweet, loving Genevieve—and Ezekiel.

The bastard had the barrel of his gun pressed against the side of her head and was slowly moving toward a covered buggy someone had hitched to the post in front of the general store.

Adam felt as though he'd just been run over by a train. His knees almost buckled, his heart seemed to drop, and he was filled with rage.

"No." The word was issued in a low, guttural moan.

Ryan was slowly edging toward Ezekiel. His attention was fully directed on him. Adam also moved closer, but his focus remained centered on Genevieve.

He knew she had to be terrified, but she was valiantly trying to hide her fear from him. Then he saw the tears in her eyes, and his rage became uncontrollable.

He wanted to kill the bastard with his bare hands. He first had to get rid of the gun threatening

Genevieve. Ezekiel's left arm was wrapped tightly around her waist, and he was using her as his shield as he slowly pushed her forward to the side of the buggy. His right hand held the gun up against her head, and his finger was on the trigger.

"It's going to be all right," Adam whispered so low she couldn't possibly hear him.

As if by some unspoken joint decision, both Adam and Ryan began to fan out in a V as they continued toward their prey. They were about fifteen feet away from Ezekiel when he shouted an order to stop.

"If you take another step, I'll kill her," he screamed.

Adam could hear the panic in his voice and see the wild, frantic look in his eyes. Like a cornered rat, he was ready to strike. Adam didn't want to do anything that would provoke him into accidentally squeezing that trigger.

He'd never been so damned scared in his whole life. He hadn't told Genevieve he loved her, and, God, he needed to say the words at least a million times. He wanted to grow old with her and tell her each and every day for the rest of their lives how much she meant to him.

"Let her go, Ezekiel," Adam pleaded.

"I'm getting out of here, and no one's going to stop me," Ezekiel screeched. "I've got nothing to lose, and if you want her to live, you won't follow me."

"I can't let you take her with you," Ryan shouted.

Ezekiel turned his head toward the marshal. "I'll kill her," he yelled. "If my hand starts shaking, this gun's going to fire, and it'll be your fault. Both of you throw your weapons down and turn around."

"No." Genevieve screamed. "He'll shoot you in the back. Don't do it, Adam."

"Shut your trap," Ezekiel hissed. "You brought this trouble on yourself. If you hadn't stolen my money . . ."

"It's Thomas's money, not yours. I'm taking it back to him."

"From your grave?" Ezekiel taunted. "You don't think I'll let you live, do you? You're a naive fool, Genevieve. Stop struggling," he snapped when she tried to push his arm away.

"Let her go," Adam implored.

The anguish she heard in his voice broke her heart. "I'm so sorry," she whispered.

"I told you to drop your guns," Ezekiel demanded once again.

"I can't do that," Ryan called out.

Adam was slowly advancing to the left while Ryan angled to the right. The lawman extended his arm and aimed his gun at Ezekiel and Genevieve. Adam knew what Ryan was going to do. His blood ran cold. He looked at Ryan and saw that his blue eyes had turned as cold as frost.

"Don't do it," he shouted.

"I can take him."

"No."

Ryan ignored him. He kept moving forward, trying to get a clear shot. He knew he'd get only one chance, and if Ezekiel's death wasn't instantaneous, Genevieve would also die.

"Stay where you are," Ezekiel warned. His eyes darted back and forth between Adam and Ryan as he slowly pushed Genevieve closer to the buggy.

"This is your last chance," Ryan called out. "Let her go now, or I swear to God I'll drop you where you stand."

Adam now wanted to kill Ryan. How dare he gamble with Genevieve's life? Adam didn't care that Ryan was right. He too knew Ezekiel would kill her as soon as he had the opportunity, but if Ryan's shot missed, or if Ezekiel's finger flinched, Genevieve would pay the price.

He couldn't let that happen. If keeping her safe

meant that he had to die, then that was what he was going to do.

Adam started running toward the buggy, deliberately trying to draw Ezekiel's fire, and when he was about five feet away, he went for his gun.

The bastard fell for his ploy. Adam had made himself an easy target, and the temptation was too great for Ezekiel to resist. He swung his gun away from Genevieve and took aim.

Ezekiel was dead before he could squeeze the trigger. As soon as the barrel moved away from her head, Ryan fired. The bullet cut through the center of his forehead. Adam's bullet entered Ezekiel's forehead a hair's width away from Ryan's.

The force lifted Ezekiel off his feet and hurled him backward. Genevieve was thrown to one side. She screamed as she fell and then began to sob.

She had thought that Adam was about to die when he put himself in front of Ezekiel, and the terror and desolation she had felt in that terrifying moment had nearly destroyed her.

Adam gently lifted her up. She threw herself into his arms and continued to sob uncontrollably.

He held her tight and tried to get rid of his rage so that he could comfort her.

Both of them were shaking. "I thought I had lost you," he whispered gruffly.

"It's all my fault. You should have stayed at Rosehill. . . . I almost got you killed, and if you had died, Adam, I couldn't have gone on. I . . ."

"Hush, sweetheart. It's over now."

She jerked away from him. "How dare you take such a chance," she cried out. "How dare you . . ."

She couldn't go on. Her sobs were heart-wrenching. He pulled her back into his arms and hugged her tight. He never wanted to let go.

"Don't cry, my love. Don't cry." He bent down and kissed the top of her head. "You were very brave."

"No, I wasn't. I was scared."

"I was scared too," he admitted.

She looked up at him, her eyes wide. "You? Scared? I don't believe you. Nothing scares you."

He laughed. The sound was harsh to his ears. He used his thumbs to wipe the tears away from her cheeks and laughed again. "My hands are still shaking. I swear to you, Genevieve, no one is ever going to hurt you again."

She was safe. He kept telling himself that in hopes that he would get over his anger. He was still so furious with Ryan he could barely control himself.

She knew she would never be able to stop crying if she didn't move away from him, but she wanted to cling.

"I almost got you killed," she said again. "Ezekiel was right. He told me I was a naive fool, and I was, Adam. I've been nothing but trouble to you. No man deserves such heartache."

He grabbed hold of her chin. "You didn't make me follow you," he reminded her, and before she could argue the point, he kissed her.

She promptly burst into tears again. He was such a good man, and he was being so terribly sweet to her.

She looked down at Ezekiel and cringed inside. Adam took her hand and pulled her away. He was staring at the lawman who had helped him only minutes ago.

"Is he Daniel Ryan?" she asked.

"Yes."

"Does he still have Cole's compass?"

Adam nodded. "He told me he'll bring it to Rosehill," he said.

"Why are you glaring at him?"

"He took a terrible risk with your life. If he had missed . . ."

"Don't think such thoughts. I'm thankful, and I must go to him and tell him so."

"No."

"Ezekiel told me he was going to kill me because I had caused him so much trouble."

"Ryan should have waited," he stubbornly insisted.

The marshal heard his comment. "I knew what I was doing, Adam."

"The hell you did. You should have let me—"

Before he could continue, Ryan cut him off. "You were too emotionally involved. I wasn't."

"You're a coldhearted bastard."

Ryan stepped closer. "Damned right I am."

"You could have killed her. If Ezekiel had moved an inch or flinched, you would have gotten her."

"I waited for my shot."

"The hell with that logic."

Genevieve couldn't figure out what was happening. The two men who had worked together to save her life just moments ago were now acting as though they wanted to kill each other. It didn't make any sense. "Gentlemen, if you will please calm down and—"

"You didn't care if she lived or died. What kind of marshal are you? You're supposed to protect citizens, not shoot at them."

Adam shoved Ryan in the chest. Ryan shoved back. "I cared about her, but I don't happen to love her, and you obviously do. Understand the difference? Look at your hands. I'll bet they're still shaking."

"They're shaking all right, with the need to put my fist through your face. I swear . . ."

Out of the corner of his eye Adam saw Lewis, the man he'd struck unconscious, come up on his knees. He also saw the gun in his hand. At the same instant, Ryan spotted the flash of metal. Both men turned simultaneously and fired.

Adam's bullet shot the gun out of Lewis's hand. Ryan's bullet blasted a hole in his chest. Lewis swayed backward, then pitched forward to the ground.

Genevieve's hand flew to her throat. It happened so

fast she didn't even have time to scream. Neither Adam nor Ryan seemed much perturbed by the interruption. They both watched Lewis for several seconds to make sure he wasn't going to move, then turned back to each other and resumed their heated debate as though nothing out of the ordinary had happened.

She took a step back from them and bumped into Sheriff Norton.

"How can they be so callous? They just killed a man." Her voice shook with emotion, and she was trembling from head to foot.

"It seems to me that man needed killing. He would have gotten one of them if they hadn't shot him, so you shouldn't be fretting about it."

"Why are they arguing?"

"Ah, it's just their way of letting off steam. I saw the whole thing from Barnes's porch. You had both of them real scared, ma'am. If that gun had gone off up against your head, it would have been a real mess."

The sheriff nudged Ezekiel's leg with the tip of his boot. "He don't look so dangerous now, does he?"

Genevieve wouldn't look at the dead man. She turned back to Adam just in time to hear him tell Ryan he should have tried to negotiate with Ezekiel.

"I never negotiate with criminals," Ryan countered. "You can get as mad as you want, but after you calm down, you'll admit I was right to do what I did. I told you I wouldn't miss. I didn't, did I?"

"You're that cocksure of yourself?"

"No, I'm that good," Ryan boasted. "You made it easy by becoming his target. That was a stupid move, by the way."

Adam took exception to his comment. He shoved Ryan again. The lawman didn't budge.

Genevieve desperately needed to sit down for a few minutes. Her heart was racing, and her legs were so weak she could barely stand up. She headed back to the jail with the sheriff at her side.

"I almost got Adam killed," she confessed in a pitifully weak voice.

The sheriff latched onto her arm. "You're trembling like a leaf," he remarked. "It weren't your fault your man almost got shot."

"Yes, it was my fault. He was living a peaceful, safe life on his ranch until I came along. I've caused him a considerable amount of trouble."

The sheriff awkwardly patted her. "Now, now, there ain't no call to cry. You weren't the trouble-maker. That dead man stiffening up on my street caused all the trouble."

"He was wanted," she cried out, remembering the poster. She pulled it out of her pocket and handed it to the sheriff.

"You were personally involved with the lady," Ryan accused loud enough for Genevieve to overhear.

"Hell, yes, I'm personally involved," Adam roared. "I love her, but that doesn't mean I couldn't have gotten the job done."

She whirled around. "You love me?" she cried out.

Adam didn't even spare her a glance. "Stay out of this, Genevieve. You're wrong, Ryan. You gambled with her life. I could kill you for that."

"You can't love me. I'm going to Paris."

Both Ryan and Adam turned to look at her. She turned around and ran to the jail. Her mind was made up. She would get her satchel and leave for Kansas immediately. As soon as she had given Thomas his money, she would catch the next train to the coast.

She was in such a hurry she didn't give the sheriff time to open the door for her. She ran ahead, but when she reached the cell, she discovered she didn't have the ring of keys with her. She must have dropped it along the way.

She didn't realize she was still crying until the sheriff handed her a handkerchief.

"There ain't no need to carry on so," he said.

"I lost your keys," she wailed.

"I've got them right here," he said. He moved forward and reached for the lock. "I found them in the middle of the street where you dropped them. I sure don't understand why you needed to lock up your clothes though. Did you think someone would steal them?"

She shook her head, then nodded. Neither she nor Adam had told the sheriff the money was in the satchel, and she was too weary now to explain much of anything.

The front door opened then, and Adam came inside. He had to duck so he wouldn't bump his head on the doorframe. He was frowning, but it didn't make any difference. He was still the most beautiful man she had ever seen.

"Make him go away," she whispered to the sheriff.

"I've got to have a reason to make him go away, ma'am," he replied as he swung the cell door open.

She ran inside to get the satchel but turned when Adam spoke to her.

"What's come over you? Why are you so upset?"

She couldn't believe such an intelligent man could be so obtuse. She stared up at him through the bars and tried to make herself stop crying.

"You almost got yourself killed because of me. You were willing to die for me, weren't you? You're good and noble, and I'm not worthy of your love. Your mother would never have forgiven me if anything had happened to you."

"Nothing happened, sweetheart."

She wiped the tears away with the back of her hands. "It's time for us to go our separate ways. Go home, Adam."

"Genevieve . . ."

She ignored his warning tone of voice. "My mind's made up."

Adam smiled. She should have known then that he was up to something, but she was too distressed to think about it. She sat down on the cot and folded her hands in her lap. She had just been through a horrible ordeal, and every time she thought about Adam putting himself in the thick of it, she was overwhelmed with tremors.

She didn't think she would ever recover.

Adam shut the door and turned the lock. Then he leaned against the bars, folded his arms across his chest, and smiled at her again.

"I've got you now, Genevieve."

"I won't love you."

"It's too late. You already do, or at least I think you do. That's why you were scared, isn't it? You thought you were going to lose me, and it scared the hell out of you."

"How do you know how I felt?"

"Because I was going through the same thing."

"Love isn't supposed to be painful."

"I love you, sweetheart."

She shook her head. "It could never work. We're so different from one another, and I'd drive you crazy in no time at all. I'll never forget you," she whispered.

He laughed. "Since we're going to be living together for the rest of our lives, I don't suppose you will forget me."

"I've got to leave."

"I'll follow you."

"You want peace and quiet, and I like adventures."

"We'll compromise and have a little of both."

Tears streamed down her cheeks. "Sheriff, let me out of here. I have to catch the coach."

"The sheriff went outside. He can't hear you, and I'm not letting you out until you promise to marry me. We'll go to Paris for our honeymoon, and then we'll settle down at Rosehill and you can plant your garden. I want to grow old with you, Genevieve."

She gripped the bars with her hands. He reached over and trailed his fingers across her knuckles.

"This is an adventure," he drawled out. "You can tell our children how their father locked their mother in jail."

The sparkle in his eyes was mesmerizing. She stared up at him in wonder. He loved her, and how was that possible?

"Our children?" she whispered.

"Yes," he replied. "We're going to have lots of children, and, God willing, every one of them will be as adventurous as you are. You do love me, don't you, sweetheart?"

"I love you. I've always loved you."

He unlocked the door and pulled her into his arms. He kissed her long and hard, and when he lifted his head and looked into her eyes, he saw the love there.

"You're the man of my dreams, Adam."

He smiled. "And you, my love, are my greatest adventure."

Epilogue

❧

$\mathcal{D}$aniel Ryan was Adam's best man at the wedding, and Sheriff Norton was given the honor of escorting Genevieve down the aisle of the cottage-sized church on the outskirts of Middleton. She wore the white linen dress that her mother had made for her the year before she died, and in her hand she carried a lovely bouquet of red roses.

Adam could barely catch his breath at the sight of her. His voice shook when he said his vows, but then, so did hers. When the preacher blessed the union, Adam leaned down and kissed her.

They left Middleton an hour later and spent their first night as man and wife in Pickerman's fancy hotel. Adam had a particular fondness for the town of Gramby, and the town now had a great fondness for his wife. They called her Ruby Leigh, and after trying to explain over and over again, she finally gave up and began to answer to the name.

She was as nervous as all brides are on their wedding night. Her robe was buttoned up to the top of her neck, and its sash was double-knotted. From the look on her face, he guessed it would be easier to break into the U.S. Mint than to get her undressed.

He shut the bedroom door behind him and leaned against it. She moved to the far side of the double four-poster bed, her gaze locked on his.

"Do you want to hear something funny?"

"What's that?"

"I'm scared to death."

His smile was filled with tenderness. "I noticed."

She took a step toward him. "You aren't nervous, are you?"

"Maybe just a little. I don't want to hurt you."

"Oh."

The way he was looking at her made her weak all over. Her heart was racing, and she was having trouble breathing. Loving Adam was going to kill her. The thought made her smile.

"Do you want to go to bed now?" he asked.

"You go ahead," she whispered. "I'll join you in a little while."

He tried not to laugh. "Sweetheart, what I have in mind requires your attendance."

She could feel herself blushing. "Yes, I realize that. Did you mind giving away the reward money?"

The switch of topics didn't faze him. "No, I didn't mind at all. As soon as Sheriff Norton told you about that injured man's family being so hard up, I knew what you would want to do. You have a very kind heart, Genevieve Clayborne. No wonder I love you so much."

She watched him take off his shirt and then bend down and remove his shoes and socks. He was still standing by the door, and she suddenly realized he wanted her to come to him when she was ready.

Tonight had to be perfect for her, and if it took her an hour to cross the room, he would patiently wait.

She made it halfway to him before she stopped

again. "Wasn't it nice of Mr. Steeple to send champagne?"

"Yes, it was," he agreed. "He and Pickerman are already hatching up another plan to get you to sing again."

"But I made everyone cry."

"He's hoping you won't sing your church songs again."

"I will though."

He burst out laughing. "I know."

She ran to him and threw her arms around his neck. "I love you so much."

"And I love you."

She sighed deeply and then stepped back and began to remove her clothes. He found it difficult to swallow, and when she pulled the nightgown over her head and dropped it on the floor behind her, his heart began to slam inside his chest. She was perfect.

He drew her into his arms, and the feel of her soft skin against him was as wonderful as he knew it would be.

"You make me feel beautiful."

"You are beautiful," he whispered. "Ah, Genevieve, how did I exist before you?"

He kissed her deeply, passionately, lingering over the task of seducing her, and in between his ardent kisses, he told her over and over again how much he loved her. He stroked her back, her arms, and her breasts, and within minutes, her shyness was gone.

She took hold of his hand and led him to the bed. After he removed the rest of his clothes, he eased down on top of her and shuddered with desire.

"I want tonight to be perfect for you, Adam."

"It already is," he whispered.

"Tell me what to do so I won't disappoint you."

He nibbled on her earlobe. "You could never disappoint me."

Their lovemaking was magical, and so intense she

thought she would go out of her mind. He knew just where to stroke her to drive her wild. She was awkward touching him, then eager, and when she couldn't stand waiting another second, he moved between her thighs and swiftly entered her. The pain of his invasion became all tangled up in ecstasy. He was so incredibly patient. He moved slowly at first until she was writhing in his arms, and then he increased the pace. He felt her tighten around him, knew she was about to find fulfillment, and allowed his own surrender.

She whispered his name. He shouted hers.

Spent, he collapsed on top of her and buried his face in the crook of her neck. The scent of lilacs surrounded him, and he was certain he had just died and gone to heaven.

She kept sighing. The sound made him arrogantly pleased with himself.

He finally found the strength to lift his head. "Did I hurt you, sweetheart?"

"I don't remember." Her hands dropped down to her sides, and she sighed once again. "It was wonderful."

"Then you wouldn't mind if we made love again?"

She knew he was teasing because of the sparkle in his eyes. "Now?" she asked.

"Soon," he promised.

"Every night," she decided. "We must make love every single night."

God, how she pleased him. He leaned down and kissed her again. "Life with you is going to be an adventure."

Proof-of-Purchase

1329

day to sort through them."